PRAISE FOR THE TROUPE

A page-turning thriller... Can't wait to read the next book in the series!

If you're looking for a page-turner... this is an entertaining thriller... Can't wait to read the next installment!

Full of big ideas and delicious details...

A great read... It kept me up late while I read "just a few more pages"... I look forward to the next book in the TROUPE.

Tightly woven thriller... with lots of twists.

THE UNDERSTUDY

A TROUPE THRILLER

JASON CANNON

First edition

ISBN-13: 978-1-956672-99-2 (Paperback edition)

ISBN-13: 978-1-956672-98-5 (Ebook edition)

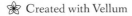 Created with Vellum

STORIES TAKE FLIGHT AT IBIS BOOKS

STORIES FOR READERS, RESOURCES FOR WRITERS

The IBIS is sacred to Thoth, the Egyptian god of learning, inventor of writing, and scribe to the gods.

They are gregarious birds that live, travel, and breed in flocks.

And they are legendary for their courage.

Visit ibis-books.com to purchase more stories and learn how to publish your own!

For my Hyde Park Pack

"understudy"

Noun.

In the theater, a person who learns the role of another actor in order to fill in as a replacement on short notice.

From the Italian *supplimento.*

To be perfectly frank, one of the most difficult and thankless jobs in the world.

"You're going out there a youngster, but you've got to come back a star."
    —*Director Julian Marsh to terrified, small-town understudy Peggy Sawyer in 42nd STREET*

1

BANSHEE WAS A STUNNING, pure-blooded, hundred-and-twenty pound Rottweiler. Even though she was a champion, held in awe, her life had been a living hell. Pulled young from the warmth of her mother. Shouted at. Choked. Shocked. Trained to obey. Trained to fight.

Trained to hate.

Her days spent in cages, bumping along in the backs of trucks or windowless vans. Her nights spent in fighting rings. Her breed's distinctive "Rottie smile" erased with every mile, every strike from a handler, every attack from a challenger.

Smells. Mountains and trees, sure. But mostly dirt and human sweat. And the tang of the various bloods from the meats she ate, from her own battle wounds, from the flesh of the other dogs she had to hurt if she didn't want to pay the price later.

She reveled in the taste of human blood, though, when she could get it. Not to eat. Not for sustenance.

For revenge.

A handler too casual or careless? Banshee would strike with

no mercy. So lessons had been learned. The humans gave Banshee wide berth, armored up when they escorted her to battle.

And she couldn't have known, but she made them lots and lots of greasy money.

She retired striped with scars but undefeated. Famous for her unnerving calm in the ring. Other dogs had to be goaded and prodded, worked into a frothy fury. Not Banshee. She understood. It was her or them. So why waste energy yapping and straining? Conserve that strength. Channel it. Focus. Wait for the moment the leashes were released. Then, like the Irish spirits whose wails and shrieks herald a coming death, Banshee would loose a howl that often as not froze her opponent across the ring and raised goose flesh on all the spectators. Banshee was aptly named.

And in her case, her bite was far worse than her bark.

She was retired early, not only to leverage maximum breeding output but because other trainers came to the point where they simply refused to put their dogs in the ring with her.

Breeders also quickly learned not to let their studs rut with her. Not since the first time when, after the expensive pit bull had done his deed, Banshee turned and casually tore out his throat. Now her litters were manufactured. Collection and injection. And her life was the crate, the daily exercise in the run, and a never-ending rotation of pups pulled young from her indifferent warmth.

Regularly interspersed throughout the monotony were the fight nights. Locked up securely in her giant crate in her tiny closet room just off the killing floor, she could hear the handlers screaming and dragging the dogs into a frenzy. Could hear the entire structure around her echoing and vibrating with the stomps and cheers of smelly, stupid humans.

Tonight was a fight night. It had gone as usual. Banshee had been paraded around the dirt ring, injured yet another handler, exited to thunderous applause. She lied down in her crate, ignored her water dish, relished the taste of human blood still bitter in her jaws.

Same old same old.

But then something changed. Even through the thick door to her solitary confinement, she sensed something in the air. Odd smells.

But so what. She didn't care. Not even this strange night when, long after the fights had ended, the humans started screaming again. In pain rather than excitement. That was mildly interesting.

She drank some water. Looked up when the unmistakable sound of a dog attacking something it hated rattled in through the vents.

Then it got quiet. Eerily so.

But again. So what.

Banshee circled and settled, was almost asleep when the door to her room opened. She glanced over. Sniffed the air. Two unfamiliar humans stood framed in the doorway. She humphed and laid her head back down.

She didn't know them, but she already hated them.

Because Banshee hated everyone.

Wouldn't you?

2

FORMER GREEN BERET STAN KANE had a soft spot in his heart for animals. All animals. He didn't hunt them. Didn't eat them. Didn't hurt them.

Except mosquitoes. He would swat the ever-loving snot out of mosquitoes. Mosquitoes were the cause of more human suffering and death than any other organism in history. Even in modern times, over a million people a year were killed by mosquitoes. If they served any purpose on this green earth, Stan couldn't see it.

But all other animals? He loved them. The ugly ones. The slimy ones. Even the dangerous ones. Especially the dangerous ones. Ninety-nine times out of a hundred, if an animal hurt a human it was the human's fault. Dangerous animals were just misunderstood animals.

Especially dogs. Former Green Beret Stan Kane adored dogs. He'd had them growing up. Fairer to say he had an ever-rotating pack that followed him all over the family farm. He also worked intimately with dogs on his deployments. He hadn't had a dog in a few years, though. He told himself it was because of his transient lifestyle with the Troupe. Because he didn't have trustworthy neighbors near enough to his North Carolina mountain cabin who could look after a dog when he was out on a performance. But really he avoided bringing another dog into his life because his heart was too raw.

His raw heart was the result of having to put down Ajax, the remarkable Belgian Malinois who had been one of the best and bravest soldiers Stan had ever served with. Ajax had survived multiple missions in the hottest of hot spots, had even parachuted with Stan out of a plane, only to be felled by stomach cancer. By the time Ajax showed symptoms, it was too late for effective treatment. Former Green Beret Stan Kane held Ajax as the vet put him to sleep, and wept for days.

Yes. Stan loved dogs. And even though he couldn't bring himself to bond with another since Ajax, he would frequent the nearest dog parks and get to know all the owners and pups, handing out treats and ear scratches and throwing balls and frisbees and playing tug till the sun set.

So when Stan caught wind of a dog-fighting ring a few hours south of his North Carolina mountain cabin, just over the Georgia border, he saw red. He was still in New York, living in the Port Morris Rehearsal Room as he packed it up. He booted up the last plugged-in laptop and went to work researching and plotting out the first draft of a script. But his research quickly hit dead-ends. He sighed. He knew he needed Adler. But Adler's help came with a cost.

He slipped on a pair of Adler's shades. Adler was a wacko, but his tech was off the charts.

"Adler, you there?" The innocent-looking sunglasses that were in fact virtual reality, night-vision, GPS-enabled, unhackable communication systems captured Stan's voice and flung it a few hundred miles through the atmosphere to the pair on

Adler's face. Bone conduction speakers created crystal clear conversation.

"Stan the Man! How goes it with you this fine eve?"

"I need intel."

"I'm great, thanks for asking. Getting ready for a date, actually. Shaving and plucking."

A silent stand-off. The cost. Adler believed in social niceties.

"What's this one's name?" Stan asked.

"Neil! I think you'd like him, Stan. Our first date? Oh my holy god, he took me to hear this punk-bluegrass fusion band—"

Stan ran web searches and studied maps as Adler described in exquisitely vivid detail how his first date with Neil had gone.

The intel better be worth it.

"—and he even made me banana pancakes in the morning!"

"Sounds like a keeper."

Adler went "mmmmmmmmmm."

"So. Intel."

"You got it, my man. Hit me."

Stan hit him with what little he had. Dogfighting venue known in underground circles as simply the Pit. Housed in a hunting cabin that had expanded through multiple remodelings and additions to include a breeding compound. High up in the north Georgia mountains near a strange little town called Helen. Helen had reimagined itself as a Bavarian alpine village in the late 1960s as a way to resurrect the economic prosperity it had lost as the lumber industry tanked. Third most visited town in Georgia, but fewer than 600 full-time residents. Lots of nearby vineyards and hiking. And all the buildings with south-German-styled facades.

Adler whistled. "I gotta check this place out. Looks like their Oktoberfest friggin' rocks."

"Adler. Focus."

"Right right right." Stan could hear Adler chewing something, then slurping something, always typing something.

Adler whistled again. "So yeah, lots of police reports here. Another ring got busted last year when cops upped their traffic stops, happened to see a bloodied pittie in the back of a truck."

Stan's silence burned.

"You still there, my man?"

"I'm here, Adler."

"It's just you went spooky quiet like you do when you're considering something rash."

"We're ahead of the authorities on this one, Adler. I need a location."

"And if I give it to you—"

"You already have it??"

It was Adler's turn to sigh. "Come on now, Stan, this is me we're talking about. I know you shun social media but people leave absolutely everything out there. I've got location. Date and time of the next puppy rumble—"

"Do *not* make light of this."

Adler backed off. "Sorry, sorry, I know how you worry about furry creatures. But I worry about you. And not just cuz it's my job."

Stan was silent.

"Yeah I love you too, my man. So if I give you this location—"

"Come ON, Adler."

"—what exactly are you gonna do?"

"Undercover infil."

Adler clucked his tongue. "No way, man. You'll stick out."

"I won't."

"You can't act."

A beat. "Can too."

"Even if you could, Stan, which you can't, you're a six-foot-four ripped Black dude. You may look like the Rock, but you ain't popular like him. And this is north Georgia we're talking about. Even the Rock would get the 'what-are-you-doin'-here-boy' side-eye, if you get what I'm saying."

Stan was silent.

"You'll stick out, man."

"I'll pretend to be a big-time breeder. Make some huge bets. Money trumps race."

Adler groaned.

Stan gritted his teeth. Images of ravaged dogs assaulted him. Deep down he knew he was being stubborn, even vengeful. Definitely rash, Adler wasn't wrong. But these were innocents.

"Adler, I'm going. You know the Director would have my back."

"The Director would tell you to draft it up, run the script through development, and take back-up."

"Fine. Back-up. Where's Rheia?"

"Not available."

"What about from other casts?"

"Everyone's busy, Stan. We're laying low, cleaning up fallout from Five Points, tracking down loose Owner ends. You're supposed to be putting that Rehearsal Room to bed, remember? Hell, you just got the sling off your arm a couple days ago!"

Stan slammed to his feet and paced around the mostly empty, mostly packed up warehouse.

"Adler. I'm going. I'm putting my script together tonight. I'm driving to my cabin tomorrow. You will have a full package of intel for me by the time I get there. Then I'm gonna load costumes and props. Then I'm gonna take these motherfuckers out."

"Mmmhmm, yep, I hear ya. But just to be clear, by 'out' you mean zip-tied all pretty for the local authorities, riiiiight?"

A beat. "Yes."

"OK then how about this." Adler braced himself. "How's'bout I send the understudy to back you up?"

No beat. "No."

"He did great at Five Points."

"No. No understudy."

"Staaaaaaaan."

"I can't be babysitting some rookie when apparently I have to worry about sticking out."

"How will you learn to trust him if you don't work with him?"

"Dammit, Adler. I can do this myself. You promise me right now. You will not send the understudy."

"Stan Stan *Stan* Stan STAN."

"Promise me."

Slurping. "Fine."

"Fine what?"

"Fine I won't send the understudy."

"Good. I'll be at my cabin by tomorrow afternoon."

"How long you gonna be there at the Rehearsal Room tonight?"

"As long as it takes."

3

THE UNDERSTUDY who Stan and Adler were so vehemently discussing was at that very moment pulling into the parking lot of an Atlantic City casino.

Gideon Price had driven Adler's fully restored Volkswagen camper van. Adler had chosen to invest in such a vehicle not because he was a car-lover but because "I was conceived in one of these, baby! Love machines. You're welcome to drive it, dude. Just, um, don't go in the back. I've got some stuff in there you can't unsee."

Gideon parked, ran his hands through his short brown hair, trying to work up his nerve. Looked at himself in the rear view mirror. His hazel eyes reflected back, a hardened haunting at their edges. Bizarre that a card game could get to him after what he'd gone through with the Troupe the last few months. But dopamine is dopamine.

He got out and took in the Boardwalk. The inexorable Atlantic crashed. The Observation Wheel offered tourists to the heavens and bathed the Steel Pier with flashing patterned light.

Gideon walked through the casino door. A cage cashier magically transfigured his bankroll into a clear plastic rack of colorful clay chips.

His nerves jangled with the cacophonous bells, whistles, cheers, and curses. He wove through slot machines and game tables lined up on loudly patterned carpet that gave off the aroma of drunken fun and tense desperation. Slingshotted around a roulette wheel to arrive at the poker room. He looked longingly at a $1/$2 no-limit table but heard Adler chiding him. *You gotta play for real, dude. Tangible stakes. If it can't hurt you, you won't learn.*

So Gideon trudged to an open seat at the nearest $2/$5 table, acknowledged the nod from the dealer, and sat down. He arranged his chips into color-coded stacks, leaned back, slipped on sunglasses, folded his hands in his lap, put an oblivious expression on his face, and watched.

These were run-of-the-mill sunglasses, not a pair of Adler's shades. Adler had insisted.

"No no no. Do not wear my shades. I'll be way too tempted to tune in and watch and then—I know myself—I'd start kibitzing like crazy. You've gotta do this on your own, my young apprentice. But here's something I *can* do."

Adler pulled his treasured replica Gandalf staff from its place of honor above the mantle. Tapped Gideon on both shoulders.

"I dub thee ready to be taken to the cleaners. May all your Balrogs be bogus."

4

How POKER FIT into Troupe training Gideon wasn't entirely sure. But he was in between acting gigs and had put teaching on hold till he saw how his stint with the Troupe played out. Yet no one seemed interested in providing him clarity. A couple days into setting up the new Rehearsal Room, Rheia had headed off somewhere to follow some lead. Stan didn't want his help packing up the old Rehearsal Room. The Director was busy supervising all the casts. That left him loads of time to train with Adler.

So Gideon had walked down the stairs of the new Rehearsal Room in Cottage City, a D.C. suburb nestled against the Anacostia River. Quaint houses on tree-lined streets. Far less elbow room than the Port Morris warehouse, but bedrooms on the second floor, a real kitchen, heck even a back yard for grilling. It felt almost normal. Except for the scads of monitors and wires running all over the living and dining rooms, and the combat training equipment in the basement.

Gideon stepped over a dissected laptop on the bottom step, turned the corner to enter the kitchen, discovered a poker table set up and Adler lying on his back with his lanky legs up the wall. Shamrock boxers. *Poltergeist* t-shirt. Ubiquitous bathrobe.

"Wild Bill! Just getting the blood back into my head. Grab some coffee and pull up a seat."

Coffee grabbed and seat pulled up, Gideon asked, "Wild Bill?"

"Dead man's hand, dude." Adler rolled to his feet, shook his whole body, cracked an energy drink, and joined Gideon at the poker table, which in addition to chips and cards was laden with a cornucopia of snacks. "Two pair, aces and eights, kablamo! Help yourself, dude."

Gideon picked out the one piece of fruit buried in Adler's pile of "breakfast."

"This mornin' I'm gonna learn ya some game theory!"

"I know how to play poker."

Adler slammed the can down. "Oh yeah?

"Yeah. I was the poker league guru in college."

Adler's caffeine-laced cackle splashed the pot.

"Oh you and your little college games. Did you also play those 'leagues' that sprang up like lice in sports bars after Chris Moneymaker won the World Series and everyone started playing online, thinking they could be the next amateur to get lucky?" He tore open a Twinkies bag with his teeth.

"Actually, yeah. I did play in those. Did pretty well."

"Win a bunch of bar tabs?"

Gideon felt a rush of irrational anger at the dollop of Twinkie cream clinging to the corner of Adler's mouth.

"Look, Adler, I know all the numbers. When the odds say to call, when to fold, so that over time I come out on top. You can't beat math."

Adler groaned and banged his head on the table. Cheetos and gummy bears tangled in his untameable hair.

"DUDE. Math and numbers do not PREscribe. Numbers

simply DEscribe. And they don't care about what they are describing. They are beautifully indifferent. They have nothing invested, no expectation. We're the dumb-dumbs who try to force numbers to *mean* something. You ever tracked a long-term game with someone, a scoring game? Some sort of cards, hearts or gin rummy, something like that?"

Gideon nodded. "Yeah, actually, some high school buddies and I made up a ridiculously intricate scoring system for a board game called *Aquire*. Favorite board game of all time."

"Your official Nerd Card is in the mail." Adler raised his can, Gideon his mug. They clinked. "Anyhow, those numbers, over time, start to tell a story, don't they? To describe. Who's on top. Who's on a winning streak. Carlos and me? Our thing was Yahtzee."

"This is Carlos, Tinder-ex number 7, right?"

"You hush now. But yes. That asshole once double-Yahtzeed in three consecutive games. It was like he was walking on water." Adler threw back his head and screamed to the heavens, "Screw you, Carlos! And your five fives!!!"

Gideon chewed his fruit. Adler always came around to his point. Eventually.

"But that's all just perception, dude. A narrative invented to make sense of the numbers. The numbers don't know they are telling a story. Any ebb and flow, any so-called momentum?" He did sparkly jazz hands with his long, Gumby-esque fingers. "Nothing more than illuuuusion."

"OK," Gideon said. "So how does all this help me and the Troupe take out bullies and bad guys?"

"We use these narratives and illusions to leverage opponent psychology. Flip the script. It's one of the great double-edged swords of being a human. We crave narrative, and we have this amazing power to create it, but then we can become trapped by it. We all think we're the hero! The master of the universe! So we cram round story pegs into square reality holes."

Gideon tried to unpack that particular metaphor salad as Adler swept the snack pile to one side and started shuffling cards.

"So, Giddy Gid, we play poker. Because while you may have the math down and know the odds inside out, if you can't read your opponent you've already lost."

———

Atlantic City. The poker room. The guy two spots to Gideon's right was an Oakleys-wearing pretend-alpha with shiny, gel-swept hair. Gideon's radar pinged, and he began to note Oakley's every move.

"Yeah I won this tournament last week, totally sucked out this loser on the river, but man I just knew that jack was comin'," one story went. Soon everyone at the table knew this guy's name—Brett. He abruptly lost a hand when a quiet woman on Gideon's left rivered a full house. Brett went nuts.

"Four outs? FOUR OUTS and you call me with that shit?" The dealer gently admonished Brett, who kept muttering ugly insults as the next batch of cards slid around the table, oblivious to the irony of his being "sucked out" on the river.

Gideon won a bit, folded a lot. Players occasionally quit. New players cycled right in. One guy who kept staring daggers at Brett busted out and bought back in, clearly intending to reclaim his money no matter the cost.

Gideon almost doubled his stack when he read the quiet woman perfectly and called her all-in with his flush made. She hung her head and stood up. Gideon was about to say something blandly comforting—

"That's right, bitch!" Brett hooted. "Better luck next time."

"Shut UP, man!" Dagger-Eyes snarled.

"Oh ho HO, look at this look at this, I already got your mortgage, man, you wanna give me your lunch money too?"

The tension at the table thickened. The very next hand, Brett had the button and Gideon was big blind.

Gideon allowed himself the merest hope for good cards. Taking a bite out of Brett would feel really, *really* good.

Hours of ceaseless shuffling. Days trapped in the singularity of Adler's appetite. Gideon unable to get the merest whiff of a read on the bathrobed cardshark.

Another pot to Adler. One hand pulled chips while the other stuffed a doughnut in his mouth.

Gideon said, "OK. Enough. Teach me the art of the bluff."

Adler groaned. "Nooooooo dude! That's the main reason I'm kicking your ass. You're worrying so much about what you're going to do that you aren't figuring out what I'm going to do. And one better—I'm figuring out what you, my opponent, *wants* me to do. Once I know that? Kablamo! I do the opposite."

Gideon thought back over the previous several hands.

"When I've wanted you to raise..."

"I've folded. And when you've wanted me to fold?"

"You've called."

"Or raised and shoved you clean outta the pot." Adler waved his doughnut. "Don't play the cards. You can't beat the cards. You can play the odds, but you can't force that river card to be anything other than what it's going to be."

Adler shuffled again. His dexterous fingers, the snickering cards, over and over, hypnotic. Cut.

"Figure out what your opponent wants you to do."

Shuffle.

"Then do the opposite."

Bridge.

"Just like in a fight, Giddy Gid. Take no damage. Frustrate them. Squash their will."

Cut.

"Goad them into a huge mistake. Then exploit that mistake to incapacitate."

Shuffle.

"Your goal is to drive that person away from the table. To make him regret ever sitting down."

Bridge.

"To make him think twice before he ever sits down again."

The cards didn't cooperate. Ten-six off-suit. Nothing with which to wallop Brett.

Everyone folded except Dagger-Eyes, who called.

Brett raised. As he had done every time on the button. Pushing. Overt bullying. But this raise was larger than usual. Gideon smelled weakness. He called.

Dagger-Eyes cursed. He should have known better. He folded. Leaving Gideon heads up with Brett for the first time. The flop missed Gideon entirely. "Your bet," the dealer said.

Gideon waited. He breathed.

Brett riffled chips. Chewed gum.

Gideon waited.

"C'mon, dickwad, action's on you, you've done jack shit all game."

Gideon waited. The entire table shifted. The temperature rose. Gideon waited.

"DUDE!" Brett looked at the dealer. "You gonna do your job?"

The dealer cleared her throat. Just before the dealer spoke, Gideon reached out and gently tapped the felt. Brett groaned.

"All that for a fucking CHECK?" He shoved in a pot-sized bet. "Take your check to the bank, amiright?" And Brett started in on another story of Brett's poker prowess.

Gideon resisted the urge to check his hole cards. The ten-six of course was still a ten-six. He watched Brett, who radiated confidence.

"Might as well fold now, dickwad!"

But if Brett was so sure his hand was good, wouldn't he try to lure Gideon into calling? So as to extract more chips? He wants me to fold, so...

Do the opposite.

Gideon casually pushed in chips. Brett's chatter escalated. "You just keep making mistakes, man!"

The dealer burned a card. Turned fourth street. The board paired fives, but still nothing for Gideon, not even a draw.

He gazed blandly at Brett.

"OK, here we go," Brett huffed and puffed. Jabbed a finger at the dealer. "Put him on the clock—"

Gideon had already tapped the felt.

Brett flexed as he double-fisted two stacks of chips and splattered them toward Gideon.

"Sir, please don't splash the pot," the dealer muttered as she started stacking and counting.

"Whatever, this prick's gonna fold anyway."

Gideon waited for the count. Brett glared. As the dealer announced the official size of the bet—and it was *big*—Brett leaned forward, pulled off his Oakleys, and growled, "Look into my eye!"

Gideon almost snorted. Now it was crystal clear. Anyone

with a hand that strong would want to milk as much money as possible. And anyone with a hand that weak would absolutely try to intimidate their opponent into folding.

So what happens when the bully gets bullied?

————————

Shuffles. Bridges. Chips. Pots.

Gideon started to win a couple hands. Or at least not lose his shirt.

Adler said, "It's not enough to identify what your opponent wants you to do. You can't just ho-hum-do-the-opposite and call it good. Style matters."

"Style?" Gideon asked.

"Yeah. You're our resident expert theatre arteest. Bring that theatricality to bear, dude. HOW you do the opposite is EVERYthing."

"Leverage the pressure."

"Exactly. You familiar with Bruce Lee's adage 'be water'?"

"What is the obsession with Bruce Lee quotes around here? You, Stan..."

Adler went serious. "He is The Master." Adler belched. "Water assumes the shape of its container, yeah? Water ADAPTS. It has no prescribed dimension. It follows its own set of rules, constantly shifting to what each moment needs. It doesn't push or pull. It flows. It goes around impediments, or over, or under. But if just a trickle gets inside a rock and freezes? Dude. The rock *shatters*."

Adler's fingers flicked like a metronome. Hole cards appeared like magic.

"So. Dude. There will come a time when your opponent, frustrated by your repeated refusal to do what he wants, will overreach. Present cracks for you to water-wriggle in. That's when you raise, or when you tempt your opponent into raising back when you've got the nuts. Same thing in a performance or a fight. Do not give your scene partner what they want. Until the moment you have full control. Then?" Adler grabbed one of the empty energy drink cans and crunched it in his fist. "Kablamo."

Be water.

Brett had just revealed a crack. Time to wriggle in and freeze.

Gideon spoke in a bored tone. "All in."

Brett's teeth snapped. The table inhaled and held its breath. Gideon deliberately placed his remaining stacks into the middle. Then sat back to watch Brett's inflated ego do battle with his self-preservation instinct.

Even if he lost this hand, Gideon knew he had learned Adler's lesson. The cards and money meant nothing. He had stripped Brett bare.

"What the fuck, man, there's no way you hit those fives. You hit those fives? You called me pre-flop with a fuckin' FIVE?" Brett riffled chips violently, hemmed and hawed. Talked through the entirety of the hand multiple times, trying to work up the courage to call. Or, more likely, saving face on his bluff gone bad.

The chips sat there, implacable, a multi-colored mountain, the largest pot of the night.

Gideon waited. Drip, drip, drip. Dagger-Eyes finally said to the dealer, "Hey, put this jerk on the clock." Brett spat venom at Dagger-Eyes, who shark-grinned back.

Brett finally muttered, "Sits there all night, playing pussy poker, gets lucky, no skill, no idea what he's doing, whatever." And mucked his hand. Fold.

The table almost burst into applause. The dealer gave Gideon the smallest smile as she handed off the pot. Gideon picked up his meager ten-six.

"Hey. Brett."

The cards sailed lightly through the air and landed face up right next to the Oakleys. Brett stood up so fast he knocked his chair over. And now the table DID celebrate.

"Oh yes!"

"Whaaaat?"

"He read you like a book!"

Brett thundered. "TEN-SIX OFF-SUIT??" Other tables turned to look. The pit boss flicked a finger and a security guy made his way over. It took another couple minutes for the dust to settle to the point where the dealer could even begin the next hand.

Gideon hung out, played tight, left Brett's carcass for everyone else to pick at. Brett quite expectedly went on tilt, over-betting and losing, busting out just three hands later to Dagger-Eyes, who got his mortgage back. With interest.

5

GIDEON CASHED out and strolled the Boardwalk, a bounce in his step. Treated himself to an ice cream cone.

And basked in the *feeling*.

As an actor, he had experienced the rush of walking on stage in front of thousands of people. The rush of opening night, sharing a brand new artistic expression with the world. Even the rush of "going up"—forgetting your lines and having to find your way back to the script with your scene partners, safety net not included.

But those rushes paled next to the rush of taking out a bully. Performing for the Troupe... seeing catharsis play out in real life rather than on the stage... the *feeling* was a drug. Dangerously powerful. Rheia warned him about it all the time.

And tonight, taking out Brett at the poker table? There it was again. The feeling.

He climbed into the camper van and swapped his normal sunglasses for Adler-shades. Adler was already there, eager.

"Final take?" Adler asked.

"Tripled up!"

"Woo! Your savings will be glad. Be sure to report your winnings."

"To the IRS?"

"Better believe it, dude."

Gideon groaned.

"Oh Giddy Gid, we do not want to draw attention. You start making overt changes to your lifestyle..."

"Yeah yeah. Hey, didn't you have a date tonight? With Neil?"

Adler grumbled and mumbled. Gideon caught something about *bunch of banana pancake bullshit*.

"He stood me up."

"Ouch. I'm sorry, Adler."

"Hey, just means you get to have a poker postmort tonight instead of tomorrow! Let's see now..."

The inside of Gideon's shades flickered and he saw a high-angle video feed.

"Whoa," Gideon said. "Is that *me*?"

"Yep. Recorded from the poker room security feed."

"I thought you weren't going to watch me!"

"Nooooo I said I wasn't gonna kibitz. And once Neil bailed I had nothing else to do but spy on you. You see a camera, I'm seeing you."

"So how'd I do? You think Stan and Rheia will be proud?"

Adler cackled. "You're like a puppy, so eager for an ear scratch."

"I TRIPLED UP. I read that jerk perfectly."

"Ah yes. The charming Brett." Adler fast-forwarded the footage. Gideon watched himself toss the ten-six across the table. Grinned as he relived Brett blowing a gasket.

Adler interrupted his reverie. "I would have been disappointed if you hadn't taken him out. He was transparent."

Gideon deflated. Grumbled and mumbled. Adler caught something about *bunch of Bruce Lee bullshit.*

"C'mon now, Giddy, not every scene partner will be so obvious. You did good to recognize him quick, but you then targeted *only* him. Could you name every other player at the table? Tell me their tendencies, betting patterns, mindsets?"

Gideon realized Adler was actually asking, not rhetorically pummeling.

"Not all of them, no."

"Tunnel vision is the death of situational awareness, dude."

"You sound like Stan."

"Steal from the best." Gideon heard Adler flapping around. "I'm about to start in on another pint of Ben and Jerry's broken heart therapy. Why don't you head on back and join me? We can break down your beat down of Brett."

Gideon was about to respond when a fist banged on the passenger window. A familiar, cocky voice screamed a threat. Gideon looked over.

"Speak of the devil," Adler said.

Brett's furious face spat rage at the glass.

6

"GET out of the hippie van, motherfucker!" Brett yelled.

Gideon glanced at the side mirrors. Brett had brought reinforcements. Two buddies. Both alternately screaming and sucking on beer bottles.

"Time to boogie, dude," Adler said.

"Seriously." Gideon turned over the engine, shifted into reverse, but a souped-up Honda screeched in behind him, blocking his path. The space in front of him was open, so he clunked into drive. Another Honda with expensive rims zipped up and braked hard.

"Ummm, Adler. They've boxed me in."

"So I see. Hang tight, casino security should be seeing this pretty quick. Keep everything locked."

The two Hondas spilled another buddy and a gal-pal into the parking lot. Brett screamed taunts. Banged over and over on the passenger window. The gal-pal likewise banged on Gideon's window. The other three buddies moved into the open parking space in front of the van, drinking and laughing and yelling at Gideon to come out.

Brett's eyes bugged out. "Fuck you and your ten-six, man! I'll take that pot out of your ass!"

"He's a charmer," Adler said. "Maybe I'll loop in the cops, too, these hooligans are amped."

But then Brett reared back and fastballed his beer bottle into the side of Adler's van.

"Oh he did NOT hit Aphrodite with that Natty Light!" Adler said.

"Aphrodite?"

"You're sittin' in her. OK. I knew there was a higher purpose to Neil bailing on me. Giddy Gid, you're taking these assholes out. One improvised Troupe performance comin' up!"

"What??" Gideon could hear Adler typing furiously.

"Security feeds cut. Canceling call to the cops. There. Now it's just you and them."

"Adler! It's five against one!"

"No, dude, it's five against two. You've got me."

"Comforting."

"Actually it's five against three. You've also got Aphrodite."

"Say what??"

Gideon's refusal to engage drove the Brett gang into a frenzy. They started to rock the van. More bottles smashed against the windshield.

"Not the face!!" Adler said. "Don't you worry, Aphrodite, we're gonna make them pay for that."

Gideon clung to the armrest as the van rocked. "And what am I supposed to use for a weapon, Adler? All I've got is this half-eaten ice cream cone."

"Baton. Like the ones Rheia uses. In a sheath on the inside of your door. Palm it. Don't let them see. Then work your way in front of the van."

"How??"

"You're an actor. Improvise."

Gideon raised his hands, gestured at Brett "one sec." Brett snarled and waved at his three buds and gal-pal. They gathered in the arena formed by the blocked-off parking space.

"They're jonesing to beat the snot out of you, dude. Keep playing poker."

"Definitely know what they want."

"They want you to panic and grovel. Do the opposite."

Gideon palmed the baton.

"Remember, dude, it's five on three. Aphrodite and me, we got your back."

Brett screamed. Started to move forward. Gideon held up his hand and opened his door. Brett smirked and pulled back.

"You ever seen the movie *Ratatouille*?" Adler said.

"*Rata*...??"

"The rat that wants to be a chef? He sits on the human cook's head under the tall hat and yanks on his hair like joysticks?"

"OK?"

Adler snickered. "Just imagine I'm a rat on your head, Chef. I'm seeing everything through the shades. I'm gonna kibitz the hell out of you."

7

GIDEON WORKED his way to the front of the van. Brett and his gang hooted, gnashed their teeth.

Think like Rheia and Stan. You've studied their moves and learned their lines. Just take on the role.

Gideon leaned against Aphrodite's flattened front. Casual. Arms crossed. Baton hidden against his forearm. His blood spiked. He found himself no longer worried about the odds. Strangely, he wished there were more of them.

The feeling flooded him.

"How's it goin', Brett?"

Gideon's relaxed tone caught Brett and his gang off-guard. They glanced at each other. Brett shook his head and stomped a step forward.

"We're gonna hurt you now, man. But I tell you what. One-time deal. Hand over my money, we'll go easy on you."

Gideon "Hmmmm'd," pretending to mull the offer. Adler buzzed at his temple, "Get 'em worked up and frothy, yeah yeah."

"Think I'll pass," Gideon said. "But I have my own one-time deal for you, Brett. I'll let you walk away. Give you the chance to accept your defeat at the poker table with dignity. Maybe even learn from it, if your brain has the capacity. And I won't even ask for more money to repair the paint job on my van here."

Brett and his gang were once again baffled. Exchanged more glances. Shook their heads as if they were clearing saltwater out of their ears. "You're bluffing again," Brett spat.

Gideon leaned forward, pulled his shades down to the tip of his nose, and did a spot-on imitation. *"Look into my eye."*

Brett and his gang clucked and strutted. Why wasn't this jerk backing down or begging?

Adler's voice in Gideon's ear. "Next push, they're over the edge."

Gideon's focus sharpened. Adrenaline surged. Pupils dilated. Breathing accelerated. He began box breathing, a trick picked up from Stan's special ops training. In for four. Hold for four. Out for four. Hold for four. Take all that instinctive fight-or-flight energy—all that *feeling*—and harness it instead of being dragged by it.

"Take out the woman first," Adler said.

Gideon barely moved his lips, sub-vocalizing. "Why?"

"Show 'em you mean business. You're merciless. Plus look at the way she's moving. She's the only one with any footwork. Target Brett second. Dollars to doughnuts at least two of the posse will vamoose after that."

"Cut off the head."

"Bingo. Now push 'em and be ready for your cue."

"Which'll be what?"

"Hehehehe. You won't be able to miss it."

"Hey Brett!" Gideon called. Fake yawned. "Y'all gonna pose all night or what? If you're not gonna take my offer, then let's get a move on. I'm bored."

That did it.

Brett, the gal-pal, and one buddy charged. The other two buddies hung back and blocked off escape routes Gideon might take. Bit more strategic than he had expected.

"Adler?"

Gideon pressed one foot into Aphrodite's grill like a sprinter in the starting blocks.

"Warning light cue 1."

Brett closed.

"Adler??"

"Light cue 1... GO."

Aphrodite's headlights went supernova. Apparently Adler had installed military-grade search beams. Even with his back to the lights, Gideon felt the brightness like a physical pressure. His shades compensated automatically, so he wasn't blinded. But Brett and the gang were staggered. Complete disorientation.

"Go Giddy go! Incapacitate! Rat on your head!"

Gideon launched himself toward Brett and his closest buddy.

"No no no you misogynistic moron, take out the girl!" Adler said.

Too late. Gideon snapped a front-kick into the buddy's gut, cranked an elbow into Brett. His kick sent the buddy sprawling but his elbow impacted Brett's shoulder instead of his jaw. Brett spun away but didn't go down.

Gideon's shades buzzed with Adler's voice. "On your right!"

Gideon spun, instinctively raising his arm to deflect. Good thing, too. The gal-pal had recovered first and her fist walloped into his tricep.

"Told you, dude."

Gideon snicked the baton long and slashed. The gal-pal danced away.

"TOLD YOU. She's slippery. Handle her fast or you're in trouble."

Gideon pressed, slashing and jabbing with the baton, but even with his reach advantage nothing landed. He realized she wasn't even trying to strike, just keeping him occupied till Brett and the buddies recovered their senses.

"She always dodges left! Rat on your head!"

Gideon feinted. The gal-pal indeed dodged left, but he was ready. He pivoted and backhanded low. She leaped back and the baton just grazed her side.

The baton emitted a spark and a loud POP and the gal-pal went stiff. Twitched a few times. Collapsed.

"The hell??" Gideon said.

"Stun stick prototype. Was wondering where I'd left that. DROP!"

Gideon reacted instantly, executing a perfect theatre prat-fall to his butt. He watched Brett's buddy's huge right hook cruise by an inch above his head.

His eyes were at crotch level. *Primary target,* Stan liked to say.

From his seat he pistoned his palm forward, open-handed like Stan had drilled him, directly into the buddy's family jewels. The buddy yowled and leaned over. Still on his butt, Gideon coiled left and sprang back right, classic Russian twist, scything his elbow. This time he didn't miss the jaw. This buddy was out.

"Kablamo!" Adler chortled then choked. "Oh geez on your left, Giddy!"

Gideon was getting to his feet but too slow. One of the hanging-back buddies was bull-rushing.

"Warning sound cue—"

Adler didn't have time to finish, he just hit GO.

The lighting wasn't the only military-grade trick up Aphrodite's sleeve. The van vibrated with a deafening squelch. Gideon stumbled but Adler's truncated warning had been just enough for him to mentally prep. The bull-rusher stopped dead in his tracks, hands clamped to ears.

"Go get him! Rat on your head! Rat on your head!"

Gideon rushed the bull-rusher, captured both legs, drove forward and lifted, crashed him onto his back. Textbook double leg takedown. Gideon slithered behind, sunk in a choke, hissed in his ear, "You can go to sleep or you can hop back in that fancy Honda."

The guy gasped and tapped. Gideon released. The guy crawled away hacking. Glanced back once. Ran for the Honda and peeled away.

That left gal-pal and one buddy out cold on the parking lot pavement. The other buddy had run away after taking the first front kick. Brett was alone, rubbing his shoulder, watching it all, gobsmacked.

"Put me on speaker, Giddy."

"What?"

"Third button on the key fob. Oh never mind I can do it from here."

Adler's voice boomed out from Aphrodite like Zeus from Mount Olympus. "Brett! I may just be a van but I'll be watching you, you small-minded zit on the ass of humanity. If you don't want proof of your zittiness all over the interwebs by the time you get home, you'll pick up your friends and skedaddle."

A Star-Trek-y antenna popped out of the roof of the van, whirred and spun, and sure enough, video of Brett's greatest hits projected onto the pavement. Brett's whiny voice. Brett losing to a ten-six. Brett being shushed by security inside. Brett and his gang getting their asses kicked outside.

"Also you seriously suck at poker. I command thee! Begone!"

Brett looked at Gideon. Gideon shrugged. Brett's eyes blinked, his open mouth worked, gibberish spilled out.

The van throbbed with divine authority. "MOVE YOUR ASS, BRETT!"

Brett gathered his groggy friends. They crawled to the other Honda, groped their way inside, drove away.

Gideon got into the van. He trembled. He clutched the armrests. Euphoria tumbled him like riptide.

"If only we'd had an audience, Adler."

"Stan and Rheia are gonna chew you out for missing your first elbow, dude."

"Yeah yeah. Don't harsh my buzz. But thanks for having my back, rat."

"Anytime, dude."

Gideon patted the steering wheel. "And thank you, too, Aphrodite."

The engine turned over of its own accord. Gideon startled. Adler cackled.

"She's saying you're welcome."

Gideon shook his head. "There still better be some of that Ben and Jerry's you promised, Adler. I didn't get to finish my cone."

"In the freezer awaiting your spoon."

"Sounds good. I'll head that way soon, I just need a sec."

"You do you, dude."

Gideon settled into Aphrodite's cushions and luxuriated in the feeling. Replayed the performance in his mind over and over. The delicious impact of his strikes. The absolute power of choking someone out. Already he yearned for the next performance.

That yearning was tinged with darkness. Reluctantly he pulled back. Box breathed. Slowed his heart from a gallop to a canter.

He could hear Adler click-clacking on his keyboard back at the Rehearsal Room. He thunked into drive and exited the parking lot, found the highway. Adler's click-clacking accelerated, keeping pace with Aprhodite's puttering engine.

"What're you working on so diligently there, Adler?"

Adler's reply was grumbled and mumbled. Gideon caught something about *bunch of Stan commando Rambo bullshit.*

Click-clack click-clack.

"Hey Giddy."

"Yeah?"

"Your go-bag ready up in your room?"

"Of course. Under the bed."

"Good. I'll grab it and meet you curbside. You can eat your Ben and Jerry's on the way."

"On the way where?"

"Stan's on the warpath. We've gotta get to Georgia."

8

STAN ASCENDED the mountain road in his Subaru Ascent. He had grown accustomed to behemoth SUVs in the military, though they tended toward Chevy Suburbans and Ford Expeditions. But Subaru was known for being especially dog-friendly, from their marketing to their accessories to their partnerships with animal charities. Stan was sold.

He parked next to a motley collection of trucks and other large SUVs. Mountain roads. Treacherous. Good to have clearance and purchase.

Also these wretched humans needed the extra cargo space to transport their dogs from battle to battle.

He sat for a moment. Breathed. Gazed at the afternoon sun leapfrogging the peaks. He had to keep cold. He was truly alone on this. Down at the gate they had confiscated his phone. He wasn't worried about them trying to jailbreak it. Adler's extra security software made the passcode unbreakable. They would have confiscated any firearms as well. He noted a locker full of handguns held like so many furs at coat check. The irony of political ideology stubbing its toes on real-world ramifications. Guns, alcohol, and enclosed spaces? Better believe we'll infringe on your sacred rights. Cognitive dissonance to the nth degree.

Same with the phones. No one present at these particular events wanted anything recorded, no pics to put out on the internet. Stan wondered if he might see some famous faces slumming it.

But even if he had his phone, there was no signal this far up in the mountains. Not even his shades were able to connect to anything. So if something went sideways... no one would know. No one would come. The Troupe wasn't designed for extraction. Even though Adler knew what Stan was up to, there would be nothing to do.

Hope for the best. Plan for the worst. His Subaru was loaded.

Stan got out. Took a deep breath of brilliant mountain air. But it was stained by the sour undertone of brutalized animal flesh and the sulphuric tang of spilled blood.

The Frankensteined compound loomed above him. What had started as a hunting cabin had morphed into this twisted "entertainment" complex. Additions protruded and bulged. No attempt to match stains or paints or paneling. The building reveled in its haphazard lack of design, every tacked on room a testament to the money spilling off the backs of the dogs held prisoner inside.

A garish sign hand-painted on a jagged slab of wood hung above the entrance.

WELCOME TO THE PIT!

Snarling canine skulls hung next to the sign, scoured gleaming white by mountain sun.

Stan collected himself. The appearance of The Pit was a visceral shock. The proprietor kept a tight lid on media and messaging, so not even Adler had been able to dig up images.

Stan knew that when he climbed those cabin steps he would be heading underground.

Sounds squeezed through the building's stitches. Overlapping barks, snarls, canine whimpers. Victorious cheers and defeated groans.

He climbed. Ignored the skulls glaring down at him. Noted the positions of the many security cameras. No need to knock. The bouncer inside surely had been radioed by his colleague down at the gate, and the cameras let him know a new customer was waiting. Door opened. The sounds spilled out. Stan stepped in. Submitted to a pat-down. Took in the little lobby carved from the original kitchen of the hunting cabin this once had been. Beer and moonshine and recreational drugs at a rough-hewn bar to your left. Bathrooms to your right. Another staircase straight ahead.

"Enjoy the show, boy."

It took everything Stan had not to headbutt the grinning, bearded bouncer into a coma. For the splittest of split seconds, Stan wondered if perhaps he had miscalculated. If his rage got the better of him he wouldn't stand a chance in here.

Dogs snarled and whined. Humans cheered.

He climbed.

9

The stairs led Stan to an observation platform that ran around the circumference of the interior. A two-story house of horrors. It reminded Stan of a boardwalk, this spectators' gallery encircling the arena ten feet below. Railings kept the boisterous and inebriated crowd from tumbling down to the blood-darkened dirt floor. Music blared from speakers hanging from rafters. Handlers were out sawdusting the trampled earth.

Bookies held court at each of the four points of the compass, doing brisk trade. The proprietor had taken a cue from sports bars and wing-and-beer joints. Tightly clad, college-age women ran the little betting kiosks. Stan approached one, shouldering through the press of people babbling about the result of the last fight and arguing over the odds of the fight upcoming. He felt eyes crawling all over him. Mostly White. Some Latino. None Black.

Money trumps race, he reminded himself.

Stan flashed a fat wad of cash. The bookie—she was maybe twenty years old—took a few bills in exchange for a ticket, but

Stan saw her send loaded glances at the bodyguards on either side of her. The bodyguards puffed up and glared at him.

Maybe not.

"This place legit?" Stan asked.

The bookie squinted.

"I breed," Stan said. "Heard this was where the best bring their best."

"So you're checking out the competition, huh?" the bookie said.

"Want to make sure I'm not wasting my time."

The bodyguards took offense and puffed up even more but the bookie chuckled, her white teeth flashing through red lipstick. "Whatever you breed, boy, the Pit will chew 'em up."

If one more person calls me "boy"...

The speakers suddenly thundered the demonic violin solo from "The Devil Went Down to Georgia." The shrieking strings scratched at the high ceilings.

The bookie snickered. "And this is why your little pups won't stand a chance. Only the Pit has Banshee."

A glorious Rottweiler was brought out, striped with scars, led on a chain thick as Stan's forearm. The announcer on the PA went nuts, hollering over the music.

"And there she is! The legend! The undefeated terror of Blue Ridge... Banshee!"

The crowd swooned. Stan's blood boiled. He pocketed his ticket and stepped to the railing. Looked down into the ring.

The Rottie stood unfazed, statuesque. Looked around with what Stan could only interpret as disdain. There was no opponent, this was all just for show. A celebrity introduction to the main event. Stan had to admit the proprietor, whoever they were, understood show business.

"Tonight her son Raptor will compete in his first battle!"

A clueless moron on Stan's left elbowed him. "Literally a son of a bitch! El hijo de puta! Haha!"

Banshee turned and started to leave. Boos rained down. She hadn't shown any of the ferocity for which she was held in such esteem. Beer cans flew. The announcer goaded. "Come on, show us something, girl!"

The handler in the pit looked up. Stan followed his gaze and saw a private box perched another level up. In the box a man sat on a literal throne. The massive chair was bedecked, like the entrance, with snarling dog skulls. The man's shaved scalp was swirled with intricate tattoos. And his mouth looked... odd.

Stan took advantage of the clueless moron. "Who's that?"

"You don't know, amigo? That's the bossman, for reals."

The bossman flicked a jeweled finger.

The handler yanked on Banshee's chain. Struck her with a metal rod. The bloodthirsty crowd cheered.

"What's with his mouth?" Stan asked the moron.

"It's his teeth. *Su boca da miedo.* Why he's called Chopper.
"

The handler struck Banshee again. She looked at him. Stan recognized that look. Cold calculation.

The moron elbowed him again. "Oh oh oh watch this, mi amigo, she's put half a dozen of these *idiotas* in the hospital."

Stan reached over and squeezed the moron's elbow. Dug his fingers into nerves. The moron's yelps of pain were drowned out by the sudden roar of the audience as Banshee lunged, pulling the handler off balance. With a dancer's grace she pivoted and snapped at the handler's arm.

Stan released the moron who whimpered away. He watched Banshee. The handler's arm was encased in a thick leather gauntlet. Lessons had been learned. Still staggering forward he held his protected arm up like a shield and called for backup. But before the second handler could get his hands on the chain, Banshee ducked under the gauntleted arm and sunk her teeth into the first handler's foot. Work boots were no match for one of the strongest bites in the dog kingdom.

Shrieks of pain in the pit. Cheers of delight from the board-walk. Banshee thrashed. Stan, like all Green Berets, was expert in anatomy. That handler's ankle was broken in at least three places.

Banshee sensed the second handler about to yank on her chain. She released the mangled foot and sprang sideways. The second handler, fully committed to his pull and expecting resis-tance, found himself stumbling backward with the enraged hundred-and-twenty-pound behemoth charging. Her massive shoulder collided with his legs, an NFL safety smashing into a high school wide receiver. The second handler went flying. Banshee followed. The crowd abruptly quieted as death whis-pered its approach.

But lessons had been learned. Chopper knew Banshee. Had back-ups for the back-ups. Two more handlers burst into the pit with cattle prods and shocked Banshee's face and neck just before she reached the blubbering yanker.

Stan wished for the moron's elbow back. He wanted to break something. He tuned out the whooping crowd and watched as Banshee was corralled, held in check by the cattle prods, dragged by multiple chains.

She went still. Stan understood. Know when the fight is done. Save your energy for the next opportunity.

Banshee exited of her own accord. Regal. To thunderous applause that she utterly ignored.

10

AFTER BANSHEE LEFT it was a relentless blur of snarls and teeth and snapping jaws. Stan made large bets and small talk. Tried to weasel his way into an audience with Chopper. But it soon became clear that Adler had been right.

Stan stuck out.

He recalled from one of Gideon's acting lessons the notion of "pulling focus." Using space and gesture in such a way as to draw the audience's eyes directly to you. Well, Stan had pulled focus. But for all the wrong reasons.

The breeders and trainers and gamblers didn't believe his story for a second. Oh they took his money all right. Smiled in his face. High-fived him as dogs tore at each other in the ring.

But Stan noted the continued whispers. The glances. Even saw the bookie with whom he'd placed his first bet make her way to Chopper's box and lean down to Chopper's ear. Lipstick whispers. Chopper's jeweled fingers flicked. The bookie high-heeled away. Another jeweled flick. Chopper's personal bodyguard, a stoic woman almost as tall as Stan and thick with mountain muscle, spoke into a wrist-mic. Stan felt all the Pit bouncers on the boardwalk tense.

Shit. Cover blown. He could already hear Adler telling him "told you so."

Time for Plan B. Direct challenge. Stan went still. Stared up at the throne. His stillness vibrated. Those near him sensed danger on a cellular level and scooted away. Within a few seconds Stan was an island unto himself on the platform, his upward stare a beacon. A hush descended. Alpha challenging Alpha was something everyone here understood.

Stan reveled in causing such discomfort to such a wretched audience. Now *this* was what Gideon meant by pulling some goddamn focus.

Everyone stared at Stan staring at Chopper. Chopper noted the strange eddy on his boardwalk. Pinpointed Stan. Smiled down. And Stan saw glimmering gold and glistening fangs in that misshapen mouth.

Stan turned on his heel and descended the stairs. The viewing gallery chugged back to life. The announcer proclaimed the arrival of Raptor. Stan kept going, pushed out the front door, took a welcome breath of night air.

Come and get me, asshole.

11

STAN GOT INTO HIS SUV. Drove down the steep mountain road. They let him leave, as he knew they would. There was only one way off the mountain, and it was heavily guarded. If he showed up there? Easy ambush. If he didn't? No need to cause a scene or interrupt the fun. Let the evening's entertainment play out. Chopper and his crew knew every tree in these woods. They could pluck this large, Black, undercover spy any time they wanted. Then tear his secrets out at their leisure.

Stan was content for them to think so.

He slowed. Turned off his headlights and let his eyes adjust. He had noted an overgrown path on his way up. Likely used in days past for four-wheeling or dirt bikes. Just wide enough for his Subaru to squeeze in.

There.

He pulled off, went as deep into the woods as the path allowed.

He got out, retrieved tools of his trade from the hidden compartments in his vehicle. He checked his watch. The festivities would end soon, but then it would take time for the revelers to leave. And then more time for the hunters to find him. He climbed a tree and settled in.

Stan waited. He was expert at waiting. Military life taught you to wait. Long stretches of tense nothingness punctuated by blink-and-you-miss-it moments of absolute chaos. Nothing was more exhausting than waiting. Nothing dulled the senses more than waiting. You had to embrace the waiting. Use waiting as a weapon. See waiting as a state of activity.

In waiting you can find yourself, if you have the guts to confront your deepest fears and truths.

It was Stan's intimate knowledge of waiting that had given him his first foothold into understanding theatre. When he and the Director were first discussing the shape and mission of the Troupe, the Director had gifted him a dog-eared paperback copy of *Hamlet*. Reading it was a goddamn slog. But then in Act Five, near the end, as the Danish Prince prepared to face Laertes in the climactic duel, Stan had felt an electric shock when he read:

There's a special providence in the fall of a sparrow. If it be now, 'tis not to come. If it be not to come, it will be now. If it be not now, yet it will come—the readiness is all.

Clarity. Shakespeare came easy after that.

Trucks and SUVs trundled down the road. The show was over. Stan could hear but not see them from his perch. Low gears. Four-wheel drive. No rush. Mountain time.

Stan waited. Maintained his readiness.

One last truck. Then nothing. Night sounds. Mountain breeze. Waiting through the thickening calm for the coming storm. They would have guns. They would have dogs.

He slipped on his shades. Even though he wouldn't be able to reach Adler, the night-vision would be handy.

But an icon was blinking on the heads-up display. Somehow the shades had connected to the Troupe's network.

The most testosterone-saturated part of Stan cursed. It had been looking forward to working solo and testing its manhood tonight. But the rational and analytical parts of him breathed deep sighs of relief.

It had taken him a long time to learn to trust Adler. Though Adler was quite possibly certifiable, he was genius at providing intel. And Stan knew only too well that the best intel invariably led to victory, regardless of size or strength of foe.

Awesome tech didn't hurt either.

"Adler, comm check."

Nothing. Now waiting sucked.

"Adler. Quit dicking around."

Nothing. Were the shades malfunctioning?

Then a delighted-with-itself cackle. "Heeeey Stan the Man! How's it hangin'?"

"Where've you been, Adler?"

"I had to come down to Georgia, Stanny-boy. You were so eager to go blow your cover you didn't consider the terrain. You got no WiFi out there. That compound's entire system is closed circuit, nothing for me to hack. They even power it all on generators, man. Next time let me have your back, yeah?"

"Fine. So what can you do?"

"Well, I VRBO'd me a sweet-ass cabin up here on a mountaintop just a couple clicks from you. I'm sitting on a balcony with a fire table and a grill, got some steaks goin'. Great line of sight. Brought along my patent-pending signal boosters. Have a drone in the air. I can send thermal imagery to your shades if you like. You know. If you *want* my help."

"Sounds good."

"You've gotta work on articulating your gratitude, man."

Stan sighed. "*Thank you,* Adler."

"Oh my liege, you are so very welcome!"

"You didn't bring Price, did you?"

Alder hiccuped. "No way, Stan, scout's honor."

"What's he saying?" Gideon asked Adler as he flipped the steaks.

Adler clicked mute and hissed, "Shut up, dude! He doesn't know you're here. Just leave my ribeye rare and get into costume. You're going on."

12

GIDEON HIKED. The sun had set, backlighting the mountains with a dusky glow. But he was too winded to be appropriately appreciative of the Blue Ridge beauty surrounding him. Because there's hiking a trail and then there's *hiking*. Trailblazing. Scrambling your way over rocks and weaving through trees nowhere near the beaten path.

He relied on Adler's directions, the drone flying invisible above him and feeding real-time topography to his shades. The shades also turned his vision more and more green as darkness groped its way through the branches to tangle his aching legs.

Gideon had left Adler working on his third steak.

"I've gotta hike *how* far??"

Grease glistened on Adler's lips. "Quit whining, Giddy Gid. Just think of this as the ultimate 'shove with love.' I'll guide ya, newbie. Make sure you hit all your marks."

"God I'm sick of being the understudy. 'Shove with love,' my ass."

"Best way to take 'em by surprise. And Stan'll give you a ride back down." Adler splurted A1 on his plate, speared and swiped a marbled bite. "You've seen the intel. No way they let you through the gate. Not in Aphrodite."

"So let's rent me a truck and I go in undercover."

"No can do. Need Aphrodite closer so I can stay connected to Cupid."

"Cupid?"

"My drone, dude."

"Oh. My. God."

"I'm all about the love. So you park her here—" Adler manipulated a trackpad with one hand while stuffing more ribeye in his mouth with the other. Images swooped and zoomed on the flatscreen monitor set up next to the flickering fire table. "State Park. Start at this trailhead. Peel off at the first switchback. Come up on these assholes from the side."

Gideon studied the map. It made sense. But something nagged.

"Stan knows I'm coming, right?"

Adler chose that moment to drink deeply from his tumbler of fizzy water. He nodded and "mmm-hmmm'd" through a couple carbonated burps.

A root played prankster and sniped Gideon's boot, snagging him back into the present. He stumbled and reached out. Caught himself on a fallen tree. Leaned against the log and took a pull on his canteen.

"Adler, any update on Stan?"

Adler's voice came back garbled thick.

"This salted caramel gelato is soooooo good, dude."

"You want Aphrodite back in one piece?"

"Easy easy easy there. Stan's all good, up in his tree, waiting for the bad guys to come a-callin'. You actually aren't too far off the pass, you'll be hearing traffic heading down any minute, just off to the east."

"East. Right."

"No. Your left."

Gideon suppressed a scream, took another sip of water.

"No matter what you hear, Giddy, keep making for the compound. That's where Stan might need an understudy."

"If you still call me 'understudy' after this climb, Adler..."

"No small roles, grasshopper." Adler suddenly whistled through his teeth.

"What is it?" Gideon asked.

"You should get a move on."

Gideon screwed his canteen lid tight, pushed off the log. "Why? Stan about to perform?"

"No, but Cupid's thermals are picking up something near you."

Gideon's senses spiked. He lowered his voice. "A sentry?"

"Ummmm, more like a bear."

Gideon blinked several times. His whisper was murderous. "*Adler.*"

"It's angling away from you. Just, y'know, don't provoke it. I'll let you know if it starts chasing you."

Gideon moved, stepping as quick-quiet as he could.

"Any other brilliant advice?"

"Yeah. If it catches you play dead."

Gideon growled. "You might keep that in mind for when I get back."

For a few glorious moments, Adler was speechless.

Then a cacophony of dogs barking erupted. Gideon couldn't place it directionally, the barks were pinballing through tree trunks and off rock piles.

"Adler?"

"Stan just hit center stage, Giddy, I gotta call the show. You keep climbing."

Gideon climbed.

13

Stan watched from his blind up in the tree. Flashlight beams stabbed through branches. The thermal images from Adler's drone flickered on the inside of his shades. The men and dogs tightened their circle, closing in on his Subaru.

Adler's voice buzzed at his temples. "Ready sound cue 1."

Stan quadruple-checked his weaponry. Tranquilizer dart gun for any dogs that took an interest. Short-barreled riot shotgun loaded with rubber buckshot for the humans. Incapacitate.

He visualized the next few moments. Waiting transforming to action. Choreography. Step by step. Smooth and easy.

The readiness is all.

Six men. Three dogs.

Stan sub-vocalized. "Sound cue 1..."

He set the positions of the nine combatants in his mind.

"...go."

Stan's Subaru Ascent, like Adler's van, was equipped with many surprises. Powerful speakers emitted bursts of high-frequency noise. Dog whistles on steroids. The three dogs lunged and leaped and yowled and zig-zag-dragged their baffled handlers.

"Ready lights one and sound two."

Adler double-checked his QLab list. Lights and sound linked. "Ready."

"Go."

Stan dropped from his branch as the Subaru added honks and sirens and screeching electric guitar solos at frequencies designed for maximum human discombobulation. Blazing lights erupted as well, spinning and strobing at disorienting speed. The already confused half-dozen men yelled curses and questions at each other.

Stan moved quietly. The lone point of calm within the chaos.

Target one. Single man. Two shots. Rubber pellets pounded into his arm, then his legs. He hollered in equal parts surprise and pain before the stock of Stan's shotgun clocked him on the back of the head. His body, gun, and flashlight all hit the ground at the same moment.

Stan was already past. Target two. Handler and dog. The dog had turned and was snapping in terrified confusion at its handler. Stan didn't bother with the buckshot. He bullseyed the dog with a tranquilizer. The handler sagged in relief as his animal suddenly calmed, then he sagged unconscious as Stan's shotgun stock clocked again.

Down to four men and two dogs. All were moving. Stan's mind was a supercomputer, calculating vectors, anticipating locations, moving to where his targets were going to be as opposed to where they were. Adler's drone continued to feed thermal imagery. The Subaru wailed and flashed.

Rubber buckshot to a handler's legs. He fell. His dog turned and sunk its teeth into his calf and thrashed. Blubbering shrieks of agony. A dart whispered. The dog went to sleep with bloody jaws. The man went to sleep with a bloodied leg as Stan slithered past and popped him with the stock.

The last dog got away from its handler. Shot through the woods, circling and barking at the Subaru. Picked up a scent. Lasered along the trail glowing in its mind, evolutionary brilliance matching any of Adler's tech.

Adler saw the blurry thermal image racing up Stan's back. He choked on his gelato and spluttered into his headset, "Puppy on your six!"

Stan had just shot the gun and flashlight out of the fourth man's hands. Adler's warning caused an immediate, finely honed reaction. His body turned. His brain processed. Vectors. Velocity. Target prioritization.

The dog jumped. Stan allowed his turn to evolve into a pirouette. He caught the huge German Shepherd with an open palm on the furry chest, kept turning, redirected the flight path. The dog went vaulting past, a gymnast exploding off Stan's pommel horse hands.

The fourth man ran away, stumbling through the woods with his buckshot-broken arm cradled against his chest.

"Adler?"

"On it."

Stan hit the Shepherd with a dart as the drone swooped down, tracking the fleeing fourth man.

One dart wasn't enough. The gorgeous and infuriated animal had found its footing and rebounded back toward Stan.

"Sorry, boy." Dart two. A whimper. The mammoth landed in a drugged slumber at Stan's feet.

The drone had darts, too. The fourth man felt a tiny stabbing prick in his shoulder. Then he felt a momentary euphoria. Then he felt mountain dirt on his face as he fell. Then he felt nothing.

Two men remained. Both were whirling, screaming for

their comrades, slashing their flashlight beams here and there. One of them started to shoot up Stan's Subaru. The reinforced windows puckered but held.

Adler winced. "You're gonna need some bodywork, Stanny-boy."

Rubber buckshot to shooter's hands. Stock to skull. One man left. Stan a ghost in the woods.

"Sound three and lights two, go."

Adler snickered with anticipation and pressed go.

The Subaru hushed. Quiet. Dark.

The sudden shift to silent, dappled moonlight was in its way far more terrifying to the sixth man than all the barking and honking and strobes. He wept with fear and guilt, prayed for forgiveness from a God who had long ago stopped taking this particular man's calls.

The deepest part of his brain stem sent a warning up the chain of command. His conscious mind received it. Didn't know what to do with it. The sixth man froze.

Something was behind him. It spoke.

"Drop it."

He obeyed. His gun thumped to the ground.

"Turn around."

He obeyed. How could he not? The sixth man now knew what the dogs must feel. Those whose spirits were broken, at any rate.

The moon peeked at him over the shadow of a muscled shoulder. The only feature he could make out on the backlit silhouette was a pair of huge, silver eyes. Sunglasses?? He saw his own pathetic face reflected in them.

"Are you the devil?" the sixth man asked.

There in the woods by the Subaru, surrounded by five unconscious men and three unconscious dogs, Stan answered, "I can be."

A mountaintop away Adler cackled with glee. "Oh that one is going in the quote book!"

A few minutes later the sixth man was trussed up with zip ties, lying in the dirt next to his friends, who were also trussed up. A couple started to stir. All of them had splitting headaches and various contusions on their arms and legs. They watched the huge man they thought had been an undercover cop carry the dogs with incredible tenderness to the Subaru's cargo hold. A couple large dog crates were secured inside. He laid the animals down inside the crates, left food and water for when they awoke. He spent extra time with the prize German Shepherd, administering some sort of medical treatment before laying it beside the others.

Stan locked the crates. Then he turned to the men in the dirt. Then he waited. He was expert at waiting. Still. Silent. Stan knew he wasn't an actor. It had been proved again tonight. But he also knew the power of silence, especially when combined with his size.

Waiting was a weapon.

It took maybe fifteen silent seconds to set all their mouths to blubbering. Making promises. Begging. One mouth somehow had enough ego left to make a threat. Stan stepped forward, squatted, wrapped his fingers around the threatening man's throat. The threats wheezed to a stop. Stan didn't release till the threatener's eyes rolled up and his head lolled sideways unconscious.

"Anyone else want more beauty rest?" Stan said.

All their heads shook *no no no no no.*

"Good. Now tell me about your boss. Chopper. The Pit. Entrances. Exits. Power sources. Number of dogs. Weapons. Cameras."

All their eyes looked at each other. Vestigial fear—it certainly wasn't loyalty—lingered. Stan sighed.

"Your operation is over. Consider it already done. It's inevitable. Chopper isn't here. I am. So. You can tell me willingly..."

He stood to his full height. Pulled a steel baton from its sheath on his leg. The whispered *snick* as it flicked long seemed incredibly loud to the men in the dirt.

"Or you can tell me unwillingly."

All their mouths chose willingly.

14

STAN LEFT the men zip-tied and gagged. Double-checked on the dogs in the crates. Left them more food and water. The German Shepherd was still out but would be fine.

Stan disappeared into the trees. Ascended the mountain. Polished the plan in his mind till it gleamed.

The men in the dirt had spilled everything. Chopper had a panic room. He was already locked up tight. The Pit, too, was in lockdown, every entrance secured. If the echoing dog barks and human screams hadn't told the story clearly enough, then Stan's warning to whoever was on the other end of the confiscated walkie-talkie—*I'm coming for you*—had definitely put them on notice.

Half a dozen guards remained, four men and two women. Stan grinned to himself in the dark as he skirted the dog run attached to the backside of the cabin. With Adler's drone above feeding him real-time heat signatures, it wasn't even close to a fair fight. The only obstacle giving him pause was Chopper's personal bodyguard. Six feet and three inches of rough-hewn mountain woman. The extra barriers and biases she would have overcome to reach that position of power as Chopper's right-hand enforcer? She would be meaner than most but cool and unflappable. Could pose a minor threat.

Primary objective? Get Chopper to come out. That meant incentivizing.

Whispering his threat over the walkie had accomplished a secondary objective: prime the herd for thinning. Now, in the imagination of every guard, Stan was amplified. Multiplied. He peered from behind every tree, lurked in every shadow. Every second that ticked past pushed them closer to panic. He doubted that many, if any, had learned the skill of waiting.

This fear predictably led to a breakdown in discipline. They should have been working in pairs, should have set up crossfire, watched each others' backs, employed fundamental strategies to tilt the situation back in their favor. Instead they rattled apart, tried to cover every door and window, frittered away their numerical advantage by going solo. Spread out. Ripe.

Stan took up position inside the dog run just outside the door that led into the compound's kibble pantry and kennel. A guard was doing a sweep through the kennel. This guard was not beloved by the dogs. They barked and snarled just on the other side of the wall. Stan could feel the vibrations of their voices, pressed as he was against the wooden planks.

Stan dubbed this guard "Guard Six." Stan liked to count down. He liked inevitability. *Tragedy is inevitable,* the Director often said. *That's what makes it tragic.*

Guard Six unlocked the door. Pushed it open to peek outside. Led with a handgun, arm extended, body shielded by the door.

Inevitable.

Stan grasped Guard Six's wrist and pulled while simultaneously slamming his shoulder into the door. The edge of the door acted as a wedge, one of the six simple machines. Can't argue with basic physics. Guard Six's forearm snapped in half. The handgun released into Stan's hand. The dogs rejoiced in the guard's pain, drowning out his scream. Stan cut the scream off with a quick whip of the pistol to Guard Six's temple. Popped the clip. Emptied the chamber. Chucked the gun into the woods. Pocketed the ammo.

Stan left Guard Six sprawled in the kennel, non-mangled wrist zip-tied to a pipe. Closed and relocked the door to the run. Always leave 'em guessin'.

Stan had learned from the men in the dirt the location of the breaker box. Conveniently located near the kennel. He found it. Waited. Good holy god above how he loved waiting.

He had run an earbud from the walkie. He heard one guard ask what the hell was going on with the mutts. He heard another say "Howie, what's up in the kennel?" But Howie couldn't answer. He and his crooked arm were laid out on the kennel floor.

Stan thumbed the walkie: short short short, long long long, short short short.

A beat. Then, "Howie, what is that? What are you doing?"

Stan thumbed the walkie, whispered, "S.O.S., assholes." Threw all the breakers. The Pit plummeted into pitch black.

He disappeared into the guts of the compound, everything glowing green from Adler's shades. He listened to their panicked radio chatter until one voice finally took charge and told them to shut up. The voice in charge—clearly the huge mountain woman's—gave a coded command. The walkie went quiet.

Stan grinned. They could change channels all they wanted. He had their scent.

Adler thankfully maintained radio silence. He knew better

than to carry on his typical monologues when Stan was performing. Just feed the intel and watch for surprises.

But then Stan stumbled into a surprise neither Adler nor the men in the dirt had prepared him for.

15

CHOPPER KNEW DOGS. They were, after all, his stock and trade. He didn't love them. But he knew them intimately. Looked at them through the lens of athletic analytics, much like professional sports teams hire Ivy League statisticians and computer programmers as scouts. Each dog was an investment. Time. Money. Food. Training.

Dog flesh, therefore, was simply a commodity to be invested and leveraged. Canine blood and guts had built the Pit. Well, no, Chopper had built it, plank by plank upon their hackled backs. His position on top of the dogfighting mountain, literal and figurative, was due to his innate brilliance at identifying the pups most likely to transform into long-term gladiators.

Out of each litter of pups, you're lucky if one or two show the gift. So what to do with the others?

Some into breeding programs. Some given just enough sustenance to grow into chew toys for the future fighters, teach the up-and-coming battlers to crave the blood of their own species. Some allowed to round out a bit more and become disposable sparring partners during training.

Those with no obvious use? A waste of housing, time, and food. And Chopper hated waste. That would be poor business.

Another commodity? Labor.

Another? Acreage.

Originally Chopper had designated a particular area of his mountaintop as the bone pile. Runts, breeders past their prime, chewed-up sparring partners, fallen champions... they all had to go somewhere.

But digging graves, even a small one for a batch of useless puppies, took time and effort. Sweat equity. Even though Chopper himself never deigned to touch a shovel, one of his pack had to do it.

Graves also take up space. The bone pile over the years bulged to almost a quarter acre. Wasted. And frankly unsightly. Chopper at the end of the day was in the entertainment business. Aesthetics mattered. A few gnarly dog skulls hung artistically on his signage? Cool. But a churned patch of rotting dog carcasses? Not something someone wants to see when they are out for a good time. Doesn't loosen their wallets.

So Chopper invested. Built an enclosure that covered maybe a quarter of the quarter-acre bone pile. Smoothed the rest into extra parking, which was also desperately needed. Added more badass signage.

Then he filled the enclosure with a few key tools. Snatched up a second-hand incinerator from a going-out-of-business funeral home. Scored a sweet deal on an industrial bone grinder when a local butcher upgraded. Bit the bullet and paid top dollar for several twenty-cubic-foot chest freezers. A couple of those freezers he kept jam-packed with the spoils of deer season. A couple others rotated through sides of beef fed to the top dogs. A couple more bulged with corpses of dogs who no longer served a purpose. The high end freezers ensured no off-putting aromas.

Once or twice a month, the dog corpses were popped into the incinerator. Push a button, ashes to ashes. Huge savings in time, effort, labor, space. His pack's morale skyrocketed, too. No more hands blistered from shovels battling the rocky soil. No more drawing straws for burial duty.

All of this Guard Five revealed to Stan in short whispered bursts. Hard to talk when a furious, dog-loving Green Beret has his python arm coiled around your throat.

The vengeful spirits of every dog Guard Five had ever put through the furnace possessed Stan's voice and hissed in her ear... "Change your ways. Or burn in hell."

The python squeezed. Guard Five went to sleep. Stan zip-tied her wrists to her ankles and dumped her in the gap between two freezers. Stared at the incinerator. Heard the echoes of hundreds of howls. Tried not to lose himself to the rage in his gut blazing hotter than the fires inside that demonic machine.

He box-breathed. Four-count in. Four-count hold. Four-count out. Four-count hold.

He traced and retraced the plan in his mind. Going perfectly so far. Next? Take out Guard Four, keep counting down toward the inevitable, then spring the trap. He wasn't going to be able to break down the thick, steel, panic room door. But why bother? Chopper wasn't the only one who understood leverage and preservation of resources. The door was merely an obstacle to the objective. And there are many ways around any obstacle.

Four in. Four hold. Four out. Four hold.

His rage channeled and chilled into ice that would burn worse than flame.

Four. Four. Four. Four.

Stan went scary calm.

Four. Four. Four. Guard Four.

16

STAN INTUITIVELY UNDERSTOOD that Chopper was a sadist. He also knew that by this point Chopper's curiosity and pride would insist he face Stan alive and kicking. Therefore he wasn't overly concerned about the firearms in the hands of the remaining guards. The order would be capture, not kill.

The human ego was nothing it not utterly predictable.

So Stan shifted from stealth mode to maelstrom. He whirled up behind Guard Four, who was looking out the metal slot in the front door like a speakeasy bouncer, only this tough guy had quaking knees and sweat-slick fingers white-knuckle-gripping his shotgun. Stan palmed Guard Four's head like a basketball and smashed it forward. Guard Four's nose didn't break so much as disintegrate. His blood Rorschach-splattered the door.

Stan snatched the shotgun and hammered the stock against the wall.

"I'm coming for you!" No need for a walkie. Every square inch of the Pit vibrated.

Stan mounted the stairs to the viewing platform, stomping

hard, yelling again and again "I'm coming for you!" Adler broke his radio silence, "What are you doing, Stan?? Have you lost your mind?"

Stan ignored Adler, kept up his ruckus. And with the benefit of his shades' night vision saw Guard Three, Guard Two, and the mountain woman bodyguard converging on his location. He went still. And once again he waited. Let their flashlights pick him out. Let them scream their threats and approach.

He threw down Guard Four's shotgun and his own. They clattered on the planks.

"Tell Chopper it's time to talk."

The bodyguard spoke into her walkie. It buzzed back. She nodded at Guards Three and Two. Guns into belts. Stan stood still, palms open. They sprang forward and each grabbed one of his arms. Then the bodyguard approached and wrapped her own arm—like the root of a tree clinging to the mountainside—around Stan's neck and held him in place.

Stan realized the mountain woman was even stronger than she looked. Her threat level rose from minor to potentially significant. Still, one miscalculation in the entire operation? Not bad. Some especially shitty timing on this particular miscue, but nothing for it but to forge ahead. After all, the primary objective was about to be reached.

The lights all snapped back on. Chopper must've left his safe room and thrown the breakers.

Stan heard steps behind him. The mountain woman spun Stan around, Guards Three and Two still clamped on his arms.

And there was Chopper, holding a wicked, glinting knife. He smiled, pulling his protruding lips back to reveal those fangs and a golden grill. Stan understood that Chopper's genetics had dealt him a mouth full of oversized snaggleteeth. The school-yard taunts must've been brutal. But Chopper had leveraged genetics with extensive dental work and cosmetic surgery. Filed down and capped the most egregious teeth, sculpted his incisors into canine points, then made it all sparkle with twenty-four karat.

"You see?" Chopper said, his fangs chewing through consonants. "Even the largest dog comes to heel." He flicked his knife back and forth like a snake about to strike.

Guards Three and Two chuckled. The mountain woman's breath scoured the back of his neck as she adjusted her arm tighter across his throat.

Finally. Stan had them all right where he wanted them.

17

"Giddy you better get in there NOW!"

Gideon had never heard Adler so panicked. "What's going on?"

"I don't know, dude, but Stan's gone wackadoodle, he's gonna get himself caught or worse."

Gideon sprinted the last few steps to the entrance of the Pit. Pushed through the front door. Tripped over an unconscious body. Scrambled on all fours under the stairs. Heard Stan yelling and stomping around above him.

He tried to get his bearings, figure out the geography. He sub-vocalized, "Adler, help me out, I'm in but not sure of the situation."

"Dude. Just say 'sitrep.'"

"Dammit Adler, now is not—"

Stan went quiet. The air shifted. Gideon saw flashlight beams, heard cautious steps and screamed threats. He heard Stan say, "Tell Chopper it's time to talk."

"I think I'm too late, Adler."

The lights slammed on. Gideon's shades compensated but

his night-vision advantage was gone. He scurried further under the platform, staying out of sight.

"Now what?" he whispered.

"Misdirection, dude," Adler said. "And be snappy about it!"

Gideon cursed silently. *Think think think.*

He risked a glance, peering around a stack of hoses and pails. Saw Stan up on the viewing gallery, held tight by two men and a humongous dead-eyed woman. Saw Chopper strutting and waving a large knife.

Then he heard the sound of a large tongue lapping water. He tracked the source.

Misdirection.

Gideon moved, hopscotching from shadow to shadow, aiming for the holding pen.

18

CHOPPER LOOKED Stan up and down with a hungry gleam in his eye.

"Perhaps I will grind you up and feed you to my warriors." Chopper's speech, mangled by fangs and precious metal, was like stone rubbing stone. "They will take your strength for their own. But first you will tell me who you are and how you found me."

Stan waited. Ignored Chopper's words and focused on Chopper's movements. He'd only have one chance.

If it be not to come, it will be now.

Likely he'd have to endure a cut or two. The choreography danced in his mind, three-dimensional chess, twisting right while snapping his head back before dropping low and driving forward. If executed just so, he'd have a split second to disarm Chopper and—

Chopper grew frustrated at Stan's stoic silence. "You will talk, boy."

Boy! Four four four four.

Chopper raised his knife. Stepped closer. Stan waited. The moment approached. He inhaled readiness.

And heard a metallic clang. Chains rattling. The knife paused. Everyone tried to triangulate the sounds.

Then a massive Rottie-pittie mix barreled into the ring, barking and snarling. Stan immediately knew this was Raptor, even though he had left before the main event. Raptor's wounds had been dressed, not out of love or care, but out of the need to get him back to fighting shape as soon as possible. All eyes followed the dog and Chopper yelled something but Stan stayed still and waited.

Raptor sprinted around the ring. Leaped at the humans standing above. Snapped his frothy jaws in mid-air, unnervingly close. Landed and spun and loosed a yowl that speared the Guards' guts and broke Stan's heart.

Amidst the distraction of Raptor's fury, only Stan caught the flash of movement behind Chopper.

If it be not now, yet it will come.

"Hey."

Chopper turned toward the new voice. Saw a man dressed all in black, wearing sunglasses, and holding a metal pail used for watering the dogs.

Chopper growled, "Who the hell are—?"

But Gideon hadn't spoken to start a conversation. He wanted Chopper's face teed up all nice and pretty. He pistoned the pail forward. Popped a stunning blow to Chopper's brow. Chopper staggered back a step, giving Gideon all the time and space in the world to wind up and swing the pail in a vicious forehand.

Stan moved in concert. Seeing their boss take a pail-jab to the face had shocked his three captors into a momentary easing of pressure. Even as a trio, even with the mountain woman's unholy strength, they would have been hard-pressed to restrain Stan before. Now? Undone by the power of his waiting?

Stan mowed them down.

The only move he kept from the original choreography was snapping his head back, smashing the mountain woman's mouth. She grunted and stumbled away. He torqued his core to the left, pulling his right arm free. Immediately he twisted back, his core now a bow launching his elbow like an arrow. Bullseye to Guard Three's larynx.

Stan heard the pail ring true. An instant later he felt what must have been a couple of Chopper's caps and maybe the shattered tip of a manicured incisor bounce off his shoulder.

Guard Two released Stan's arm and turned to run. Stan grabbed a handful of greasy guard hair and yanked down. Guard Two's jaw cracked against Stan's simultaneously ascending knee. A couple Guard Two teeth rolled snake-eyes.

Stan spared a glance back to assess. Chopper was on his hands and knees, his mouth pouring blood onto the planks. Gideon held the dented pail in one hand and Chopper's dropped knife in the other.

Not bad, Understudy.

Back to the enraged mountain woman. Like her boss, her mouth was a bloody mess. Unlike her boss, she was still on her feet.

"We done?" Stan said.

She bellowed and charged like an avalanche.

Gideon knew what was coming. He'd been on the receiving end of Stan's lessons often enough in rehearsal.

Sure enough, Stan slip-stepped, captured one of the mountain woman's outstretched arms, turned in a tight twist, and slingshot her at the railing. The mountain woman's momentum was not only conserved but amplified. Can't argue with basic physics. She slammed into the wooden posts. A few cracked.

Others outright splintered. As did several of the mountain woman's ribs.

The wall is a weapon, Gideon thought to himself, recalling not-so-gentler days back in the Rehearsal Room.

The mountain woman wheezed. But she stayed on her feet.

"We done?" Stan said, a bit more pointedly.

She bellowed again and lurched forward. This time Stan met her head-on. Lunged in tight. Wrapped her up in a bear hug. This suited the mountain woman just fine. She loved to squeeze the life out of things. Humans. Dogs. Whatever.

But something was wrong. She was being squeezed back. And it hurt like hell. The arms around her were iron bands, tightening every time she gasped for breath. She could feel her ribs grinding along fractures. Then the voice of inevitability in her ear... "We done?"

She bellowed yet again and opened her mouth to bite flesh.

Gideon saw her targeting Stan's jugular and opened his mouth to call out a warning. But Stan had already bodyslammed her to the platform.

"See Giddy?!" Adler shrieked, enjoying the show via Gideon's shades. "THAT'S how you treat a damn female combatant, you sexist putz!"

Stan slithered behind the woman and gave her a taste of her own medicine. His arm sank into her throat. His legs cinched around her gut. He squeezed. She clawed. He squeezed.

"We done?" Stan said.

And still she thrashed, even as spots began to dance in her vision. Gideon opened his mouth again to tell Stan to ease up, she was toast. But then she hissed, "You better do more than put me to sleep, boy, cuz when I get my hands on you—"

BOY!!

Gideon heard Adler gasp. "Oh no no no, bad call, girlfriend."

Then Gideon blinked and somehow Stan had rearranged the anatomical geometry so that his legs were over her face and chest, pinning her down. His two hands caught her flailing arm, vice-locked on her wrist. He pulled her arm straight. Leaned back. Lifted his pelvis. Arched his spine. Textbook armbar.

You really just can't argue with basic physics.

Her elbow hyperextended. *Pop.* Joint dislocated. Her arm now bent the wrong way.

Gideon and Chopper winced. Guard Two would have too, had he been conscious. Guard Three retched through his broken throat.

The mountain woman's bellow rose in register. But she stayed down.

Stan sprang up. One hand grabbed the mountain woman's hair. His other reached out and palmed Guard Three's head.

"We're done," Stan said.

He banged their skulls together. They joined Guard Two in slumber. He wished them all nightmares.

STAN APPROACHED CHOPPER.

"Please man, please please, I got a kid, I'm sorry I'm sorry I'm sorry, please—"

"Shut up," Gideon said. He planted his foot in Chopper's backside and shoved. Chopper sprawled facedown at Stan's feet. "Save it for the judge, you piece of—"

"Price."

Gideon looked up. Stan noted the ecstasy in Gideon's eyes. This would bear watching.

"Stand down, Price."

Gideon gulped. Turned away. Chucked the pail. It clanged into a corner.

"You." Stan loomed over Chopper. "Get up."

Chopper wiped his mouth. Paused. Stan saw what he intended a split second too late. He reached down but Chopper rolled sideways under the wooden railing and dropped into the ring. He landed awkwardly but clambered to his feet and limped for the exit.

"Dammit!" Gideon started for the stairs.

"Price."

"C'mon, Stan, he's gonna get away!"

Stan shook his head, gestured Gideon over. For he had heard something. Or perhaps it would be truer to say he felt something. A subsonic, back-of-throat growl. The rumble of the predator.

Chopper picked up on it. He stopped. Turned around.

And there was Raptor.

Time froze. All four conscious beings together in that room suddenly understood with perfect clarity what was about to happen.

"Oh my god, Stan, we've gotta get down there. That beast will tear him apart."

Raptor took a step forward. Chopper took a step back, blubbered "good boy, good boy, good boy."

"No," Stan said.

"But Stan," Gideon said. "What about the Troupe? We don't kill, right? You're always telling me there's no change without a tomorrow."

Raptor took a step forward. His growl had grown to a snarl. He was hungry. But not for food.

"No," Stan said. "The beast in that pit isn't the dog."

Raptor blurred forward. Jaws snapped and tore the first of several otherworldly screams out of Chopper.

Gideon's guts clenched. He turned away. It was somehow worse *not* seeing. The sounds were horrific. He glanced to the side and saw Stan, implacable, watching.

Suddenly Stan was moving. He grabbed the knife from Gideon's hand and vaulted the railing. Gideon dared to look. Raptor was straddling Chopper, shaking his head back and forth. Canine teeth clamped on human neck. Chopper tried to fend off the relentless attack with one hand while his other scrabbled around down by his boot. He pulled something out. Halogen lights glinted on an ice pick.

Raptor yelped as Chopper stabbed and stabbed. Steel dueled teeth. Gideon could no longer tell which sounds came from which creature, so desperate were they both.

Stan stuck his landing, took three massive strides forward, grabbed Chopper's weapon arm, pulled it out straight, and stabbed down with the knife. Blade went clean through forearm, pinning Chopper to the earth.

Too late. Raptor released his grip, took a few shuddering steps away, and collapsed. Stan crawled over to the huge dog. Pulled him onto his lap. Held the giant head in his arms like a newborn baby. Stroked the blood out of the matted fur.

Gideon ran down the stairs and pushed through the chain-link gate. Stopped by Chopper, who twitched and gurgled spread-eagled, punctured and torn.

"Seriously, Stan, we've gotta call the paramedics or someone."

Stan sat with Raptor. Rocked him, spoke so very quietly to him, petted him.

"Stan!"

"No."

"But Stan, dammit, everything you've taught me—!"

"No, Price. I won't kill that man." Stan didn't so much as glance at Chopper, his attention fully on Raptor in his lap. "But I sure as hell don't have to save him."

Gideon watched Raptor's panting calm. The "beast" was nonexistent. A pink, blood-flecked tongue flicked out and licked Stan's hand. Then Raptor looked at Gideon right in the eye, as only dogs do. Gideon felt a jolt. Saw how Raptor was entirely in the present, didn't know what was happening or why it hurt. Saw how the dog was simply at peace.

Raptor turned away from Gideon, looked up once more at

Stan, and closed his eyes, secure in the safety and love of Stan's arms.

Gideon felt something scratching at his boot. He flinched back. Chopper's fingers were reaching, beseeching. And Gideon witnessed the proverbial moment when Chopper's life flashed before his eyes. Unlike the dog, the man knew what was happening and why it hurt. The man was not at peace. The man was alone. Scared. Full of regrets and what-ifs. And no one comforted him.

Gideon stood out of Chopper's reach. Stan sat holding Raptor. They waited.

The man's gurgling faded. The dog's panting stopped.

20

GIDEON TREMBLED. Stan noticed.

"First time seeing someone bleed out, Price?"

Gideon nodded his clammy face.

"You'll never forget. And that's a good thing. First time seeing someone die?"

Gideon shook his head. "My grandma. Held her hand. But she was asleep."

"Keep breathing. Four times four." Stan waited as Gideon breathed. Time is currency, and everything costs something. Color came back into Gideon's cheeks. "OK then. Let's go to work."

They carried the unconscious Guards into the incinerator room. Zip-tied wrists around pipes and support beams. No one going anywhere, but enough slack to get food and water to mouths. Once they woke up, of course.

The mountain woman stirred as they were dragging her. Muttered some threats, attempted some struggle. Stan zip-tied her tighter than everyone else.

"I'm gonna kill you, boy." She spat at his feet.

"Let me know when you want some ice for that elbow."

Stan left her spluttering. Gideon followed him into the hall. "Now what?" Gideon said.

"Now we feed and water the dogs."

They entered the kennel. The dogs went crazy. Stan stood still and waited. Gideon felt like he was in a teeth tornado.

"What are we waiting for, Stan? Let's dump some food and get out of here."

"No. We wait."

"For what?"

"For them to quiet down."

"And how long will that be?"

"As long as it takes."

Time passed. The barking did not abate.

Stan said, "Price, maybe it's best you step outside."

Gideon thankfully backed through the door. Stan closed it, turned to the snarling mass.

"Enough. Quiet."

Through the door, Gideon heard the cacophony settle. "What the hell?" he muttered.

Adler piped up. "Stan's some sort of dog whisperer, dude."

"Where've you been?"

Adler made a shaky burping sound. "I watched that pup tearing up Chopper through your shades. I'm not good with blood, dude."

"Oh."

"Ribeyes wouldn't stay down."

"Got it."

"You won't want to go in the main floor bathroom for a while."

"I GOT IT."

A couple minutes later Stan emerged. The kennel echoed with the sound of crunching kibble.

"Now what?" Gideon said.

"Now we get ready to perform."

21

THEY WENT BACK UP to the fighting ring. Raptor and Chopper laid side-by-side in the blood-thickened dirt. Their shades buzzed with Adler's gags.

"Sorry, dudes, I gotta bail for a sec."

They couldn't tell if he made it to the bathroom in time.

Gideon felt similarly unsteady. Stan sighed.

"Head back down, Price. Get your mind right. We've gotta put the fear of god into these assholes."

Gideon hung out by the incinerator room door as Stan deposited Chopper roughly and then Raptor gently on the floor.

"They awake yet?"

"I didn't check, Stan, but I had a thought. Only half of them have even seen me, right?"

"So?"

"So we can write a script where I'm the scary one."

Stan snorted.

"Hear me out, Stan."

"Like I'm gonna be the underling to the understudy."

"No no no, Stan, see you haven't been paying attention in acting class. If we just go in there and threaten physical harm, it won't be enough. We want to break their spirits entirely, right? Incapacitated for the long haul?"

"Listen to Giddy, Stan. I'm here and ready to call the show." A wet, bubbly burp. "And *definitely* don't use the main floor bathroom when you get back."

"OK, Understudy. Sketch it out. How are you gonna scare them more than me?"

"Think of it this way, Stan," Gideon said. "If they see *you*, the terrifying monster who took all of them out solo, now taking orders from someone else, then how terrifying and powerful must that someone else be? The man who controls the monster is scarier than the monster itself."

Stan narrowed his eyes.

"Basically, how do you transform a bad cop into a good cop?" Gideon said.

Adler cackled. "You bring in a badder cop."

"OK, Price. We'll try your script flip. But if those assholes in there aren't pissing themselves within a few minutes—"

"They will be! You stay silent and follow my lead. Adler, you able to run facial recognition through the shades and dig up background, feed it to me?"

"Oh Giddy, I see where you're going—"

"I don't," Stan said.

"—and I like it! You want their skeleton closets opened up, you got 'em! Just give me an up-close view of each face first thing."

"Will do. Stan? You ready?"

Stan gritted his teeth. "Stay silent and follow your lead."

"Places, please," Adler said.

Gideon nodded and grinned. Stan could see the eagerness, bordering on hunger. This really would bear watching.

"I'm gonna mask up. Adler, be ready with that background."

"Roger dodger."

Gideon turned toward the door. Then Stan caught his breath as Gideon... *transformed*. A shift in posture. An adjustment to center of gravity. A change of his breathing from deep through the nose to shallow through the mouth. The merest hint of an Elvis sneer curled his lip. And just like that, the slightly nerdy, anxious, desperate-to-please Understudy transfigured into an Alpha male radiating intelligence and ominous intentions.

"Lights up," Gideon said. Even his voice was different. Stan reassessed.

This was going to be entertaining.

22

GIDEON WALKED IN. Stan followed. Everyone was awake. Gideon made a show of rubbing his arms.

"Brrrr. Cold in here, kids." He snapped his fingers. Stan stared at him. Gideon sighed and snapped again, pointed at the incinerator. "Y'mind?"

Adler gave a small cough. "Ahem. Stan, that's your cue. It's called improv."

Stan cursed silently and flipped on the machine. Mechanisms thrummed. Flames *whoomped*.

"There we are!" Gideon said. "Much better."

"Who the hell are you?" Guard Six said.

Gideon laughed. Crossed the room. Stan marveled. Even Price's *walk* had morphed into that of an entirely different person.

Gideon squatted. Got nose to nose with Guard Six. "It's no use, my friend. I know everything about you. And anything I don't already know I can tell just by looking."

"Good good good," Adler said. "Got 'im." Whispered intel flowed.

"Fuck you," Guard Six said.

"Yowie zowie, Howie. You kiss your mother with that mouth?"

Guard Six startled. How did this stranger know his name?

The mountain woman sneered. "He heard us on the radio. Don't tell him shit. He doesn't know anything. Chopper's too smart to let anything slip."

"You mean this Chopper?" Gideon snapped his fingers again.

Stan stepped out. Returned dragging Chopper's body with one hand. Dumped it in the middle of the room. Everyone strained at their zip ties, trying to back away.

"Well lookie there! I think we got their attention." Gideon lifted one of Chopper's arms, let it thump to the floor. Stan again adjusted his assessment. That corpse a few minutes ago had wobbled Gideon to the verge of passing out.

"We didn't do that to him, by the way," Gideon said, looking directly at each guard and giving Adler research time. "Raptor did. Karma's a bitch, as they say. Extra appropriate in this case, wouldn't you say?"

Another finger snap. Stan hefted Chopper onto the belt. The belt trundled the body into the fire. The fire hissed and sizzled. The guards moaned. Even the mountain woman blanched. The sour scent of ammonia wafted.

"Seriously, Howie? You pissed yourself?" Gideon shook his head like a disappointed preschool teacher. Looked over at Stan. "He pissed himself." He waggled an eyebrow. *Told you so.*

Stan acknowledged with a nod.

"OK, dude," Adler said. "Let's fortune-tell these morons into oblivion."

Gideon addressed each guard in turn.

"Javier, did Chopper know you were skimming from the bookies?"

"Congrats on your son's graduation from kindergarten, Marla Sue!"

"Delia, you might want to consider cutting in all your friends here on that shake-and-bake meth shack you've got going. Nice side gig."

"Billy Billy Billy, you're on Tinder, but it says you're interested in dudes. Is that right? Your colleagues know this? I personally don't care, love is love, my man. In fact I have a buddy who was just stood up, he might be your type."

"Aaaaand screw you very much," Adler hissed. "Won't be saving you any gelato."

Stan watched in wonder as Gideon, without a single slap to a face or twist of an elbow, utterly dismantled the group's resistance. Even the mountain woman.

"And you, Annabelle."

Howie gasped. "Your name is *Annabelle*??"

"You're dead, Howie!"

"Now now now," Gideon said. "Annabelle. Your Harry Potter obsession aside—I'm not surprised you're a Slytherin, by the way—I've gotta tell ya that all your good ol' boy cops and county judges can't help you this time. See, I know all their names and secrets, too. Don't think they'll be taking your payoffs again anytime soon. So here's the deal."

Gideon stood and addressed the room. His cheery demeanor channel-changed into something so steely cold that even Stan flinched.

"You're all out of the dog business. Permanently. I catch even a whiff of you in this neighborhood again or working for any other idiot breeder in the area... well. You smell what's left of your big bad boss."

Gideon waited. Let the sound of popping flesh finish the threat for him. Stan admired the waiting.

Abruptly Gideon yawned and stretched and patted his belly. "Good god DAMN I am hungry." He pointed at Stan. "Clean up here. Leave 'em some Gatorade or granola bars or something. I'm getting a steak."

Gideon sauntered offstage. Stan imagined a standing ovation.

GIDEON HEARD Stan close the door behind him, but he kept going. He needed air. He hustled through the kennel, oblivious to the dozen dogs leaping into a crated frenzy. He burst through the door and out into the dog run. Leaned over, hands on knees, gulping breaths.

"You ok, dude?"

Gideon ripped off his shades. He didn't want Adler. He wanted to bask in the *feeling*. Float in it. Swim in it. Bathe in it. Feel its power churning through and around him. It was delicious and familiar. Gideon knew firsthand the unmistakable energy when an audience shifts, whether small groups in black box theatres or throngs on park hillsides taking in Shakespeare under the stars. Audiences are temporary communities pretending a fantasy into emotional reality, and when they shift —when they collectively experience those moments of cathartic release—that energy tidal waves from house to stage and over the performers. Ecstasy. As good as any high from any drug.

Gideon had ridden those audience highs many times, but they paled next to THIS feeling. He hadn't merely caused a shift in that Pit pack, he had broken them down. Held their egos in his hands and reshaped them. Rewritten the code on their most intimate software. And days and months and years from now when they remembered his performance on this mountaintop theatre, they would shudder.

"Price."

He ignored Stan. Stretched. Breathed in the mountain air. Gazed at the mountain sky. Felt as large and powerful as the mountain itself.

"That was impressive in there, Price."

Gideon snapped to. Compliments from Stan were exceedingly rare.

"I've always thought the acting stuff was just window dressing. I put up with it from the Director and the Troupe because I believe in what we're doing. I told Adler not to send you as backup. Thought I'd have to babysit you. But I can admit when I'm wrong. Well done."

Gideon gaped. This was not only the most Stan had ever spoken to him, but the first time Stan had spoken to him without criticism.

"I guess I did save your butt in there."

"Hardly." Warm fuzzy squashed. "I was right on script."

"They captured you."

"I let them."

"Annabelle had you by the throat."

Stan snorted. "You've still got a lot to learn, Price."

"Looking forward to it," Gideon said. "Especially now that I'm not an understudy anymore."

Stan snorted again. "Oh you're still the understudy."

"What? Why? For how long?"

"As long as it takes."

"Takes for what?"

"You know your Shakespeare. Try this one. 'She makes hungry where most she satisfies.'"

"*Antony and Cleopatra,*" Gideon muttered.

"Addiction. Dopamine. Takes all forms. Shakespeare knew it. We know it in special ops. You know it. Till you figure out how to handle it? You're the understudy."

Stan watched Gideon struggle. Grounding molars. Shallow breaths. Clenching fists.

He wasn't ready. Disrupt the cycle.

"Let's go, Price."

"Where?"

"A ways down the mountain. Put on your shades."

Gideon slipped them on. "What now?"

Adler said, "That was just the matinee, dude. It's a two-show day."

Stan held up the keys he had pulled from Chopper's pocket. "Another audience to impress."

They took Chopper's F-150 down to Stan's Subaru. Hammered out logistics on the way.

"After this show, Adler, you get up here and help Price load the dogs."

"Hold up, man. We're taking them?"

"Why not leave them for the authorities?" Gideon said. "We're calling this in, right? Cops'll come and take Annabelle and her crew, they can take the dogs, too."

Stan shook his head. "This area is known for high kill shelters. These dogs don't have a prayer in the system. They're damaged, need time and patience to rehabilitate. PTS isn't just a human condition. They'll be put down without a second thought. Hard to find homes for 'killers.' I know good people. Veterans and dogs bond fast. We're taking them."

"But Aphrodite is delicate!" Adler whined. "She can't handle fur and poop, much less mountain roads."

"So rent a goddamn truck, Adler. Move your ass."

Adler grumbled and mumbled. Stan and Gideon both caught something about *have to do everything around here.*

Down at the Subaru, the zip-tied men were angry and frisky. But Gideon reprised his role, used Adler's info to break their spirits without breaking a sweat. They tossed the men into the truck bed, drove it and the Subaru back up to the Pit. Marched them into the incinerator room for a reunion with their colleagues. Left a pile of jerky and Cliff bars within reach. Headed to the kennel to prep for Adler's arrival.

Stan realized a dog was missing. Sniffed a trail back to the fighting ring. Gideon followed. The path diverged at the chain-link gate.

"This is where I released Raptor," Gideon said. "Holding pen that way." He pointed right.

Stan nodded. Looked left. Picked out a shadowed path weaving under the platform.

"Like being under the high school bleachers," Gideon said.

They followed the path. Came to a heavy door covered with hooks from which hung all the prods and chains and protective equipment Stan had seen earlier. Lessons had been learned.

Stan pushed the door open. The small room was dark. It stank of blood and shit. In the dim light he could just make out a massive cage, bolted to the floor and wall.

They heard breathing.

"What the hell?" Gideon said.

Stan shook with suppressed fury. If Raptor hadn't already mauled Chopper, Stan may not have been able to stop himself.

"Solitary confinement," he said. "Trying to break her. But you haven't broken, have you, girl?" He reached up and pulled a small chain. A naked bulb flickered on. Its meager light reflected in a pair of dark eyes.

24

BANSHEE LIFTED her head as the door opened. Sniffed the air. Two unfamiliar humans stood framed in the doorway. She humphed and laid her head back down.

She hated them.

The smaller human smelled afraid. Typical. They all stank of either fear or hatred, those most kissingest of emotional cousins.

But then the larger human spoke. Of course she didn't understand his words, but she heard something odd in his tone. Compassion? Another word she didn't know, but as he spoke she could feel his eyes on her, his energy and intention. And they were warm, with no expectation, no demand. She lifted her head again, sniffed more deeply.

"She's coming, too."

"Wait, what?"

"With me. You and Adler will take the rest, but she's coming with me."

"That's a German monster in there, Stan. How do you expect—?"

"I'll befriend her. And Rottweilers aren't originally German."

Stan approached the crate. A growl began in the giant dog's throat. Stan stopped. Gideon backed up a step. Stan spoke calmly, the meaning of his words for Gideon, but the feeling of his words for Banshee.

"Rotts settled in Rottweil, Germany, but only after their ancestor came up with the Roman legions." Another step. The growl increased. Gideon felt the vibration from the animal's massive chest through the ground, up his legs.

"The Romans trusted this dog to herd the cattle, guard the camp." Another step. Banshee sprang to her feet. Her growl shook the tiny room. "Then the people in the forests who would become the Germans trusted this dog to herd, to pull sleds of meat to market. They'd put their money into pouches and tie them around their Rottie's necks. Go in the bar to drink, knowing no one would be stupid enough to try to steal their day's profit."

Another step. Banshee's hackles rose. She unleashed a bark that battering-rammed Gideon in the chest.

"Stan. Let the pros handle this."

"They'll put her down, Price. She's coming home with me. You go wait for Adler, load up, go back to the cabin, tend the dogs and keep us off the grid till I'm done here."

"How long do you need?"

Stan reached for the lock on the crate door.

"As long as it takes."

Gideon eased out and closed the door, released his held breath. Heard a clank as Stan unlocked the crate. Heard Stan say something, but couldn't make it out. Heard the metallic squeal as the crate door opened.

Gideon backed away, expecting snarls and screams, maybe

a thud against the door. But there was nothing. He shook his head. "You're crazy, Stan."

25

STAN OPENED THE CRATE DOOR. "There's nothing you have to do, Banshee," he said. Then he pocketed his shades, turned his back to the dog, and went to the sink. Really it was just a couple rusty buckets and a hose. He washed his hands and arms.

"Whenever you're ready, Banshee," he said, still not looking at her. Just washing. Calm. "There's nothing you have to do."

Banshee crept out. Still growling, but less overtly threatening, more "keep your distance." She lifted her nose and sniffed the room, assessing. Nothing had changed but everything was different. She couldn't tell what. The human turned and faced her. She lowered into a fighting stance and amplified her growl.

"That's ok, girl. I get it. You take your time. There's nothing you have to do. I'll just wait."

Banshee was confused. The smell coming from this human... the only thing comparable in her memory was the scent of a tiny human's hands squishing her puppy face. She recalled the tiny human giggling. Everything after was sweat and fear and greed and anger.

Until now. This huge human had no scent of threat about him. No scent of fear or hatred. He lowered himself slowly to the floor, sat against the wall, closed his eyes, and breathed in a deep, steady rhythm.

She snorted. Explored the room. Always kept at least a side-eye on the dozing human. Rotties were natural assessors. He would show his true colors.

Stan awoke. Time had passed. A couple hours.

Banshee was lying on the floor a few feet away, facing him.

She awoke a split second after he did.

Neither moved.

"Good girl."

She cocked her head.

"You're a good girl, Banshee."

Something deep inside her stirred.

Time does not heal. Time simply passes. Healing is time's passenger. And gets off only when invited.

Stan put on his shades.

"You all loaded up?"

Time passed. A few seconds.

"Good. Leave me some supplies. I'll join you two later." Shades back in his pocket.

Time passed. She could tell the moment he fell back asleep.

She stretched out till her nose was able to brush his bent leg feather-light. She inhaled his gentleness. His scent fused into her memory.

She watched him sleep for a while. She heard the other human leave something outside their door.

Banshee yawned, assessed the large human, scooched forward a bit, put down her head, and closed her eyes.

Stan awoke. Time had passed. Another few hours. Dead of night now.

Banshee's massive head was lying on his thigh.

She didn't stir.

He placed his hand on her head and idly twined her ears through his fingers. His hand looked small.

He felt a current shoot through her body. Her eyes opened.

She took a deep breath and huffed it out, her entire rib cage compressing like a bellows. That sound so specific to canines—utter contentment and relaxation—whooshed out of her.

She glanced at him. Assessed. Her eyes closed.

Stan closed his as well. Scratched Banshee's ears. Fell back asleep.

Banshee awoke. Time had passed. She had no idea how much. Time was a construct unknown to her. But she knew the sun was about to rise.

The human's breath was steady. His hand was still on her head.

He didn't stir.

She wondered at this feeling of calm. She wanted to stretch, sniff around a little. But more important was not disturbing the human. If she moved, his hand would fall. Or he would awake. And he needed to sleep. She could sense his exhaustion. So she stayed put.

Banshee waited for Stan.

Stan awoke. His thigh was wet and warm. He lifted his hand. Banshee lifted her head, a thread of drool connecting her jaw to his leg.

They looked at each other. He reached out and wiped her mouth. Banshee couldn't believe how good that felt.

"Good girl, Banshee. What do you say to breakfast?"

STAN RETRIEVED the bag Gideon had left outside the door. Fed and watered Banshee and himself. Went outside. Banshee followed a few steps behind, baffled at not being prodded and chain-dragged.

Stan took a moment to enjoy the mountain sunrise and crisp air. His Subaru and Chopper's F-150 were surrounded by looping truck-and-trailer tracks. Adler had come and gone, taken Gideon and the dogs.

Stan headed down to the incinerator room, Banshee still following. He was glad Gideon was gone. His begrudging admiration for the understudy had grown, but he was no soldier. He wouldn't have had the stomach for the rest of what Stan had to do.

The zip-tied pack was sore and cranky, their food and water gone. Stan resupplied them but also took the time to rub blood back into some of their shoulders, salve and bandage a few wounds, dispense painkillers.

Not the mountain woman, though. "Don't touch me, boy!" And a torrent of racial slurs poured from her mouth.

Then Banshee walked in. Annabelle clammed right up.

The room stank of fear. Banshee reveled in it. Her tormentors were helpless before her. Her lips pulled back from eager teeth. Her growl revved and thrummed.

"Easy, girl."

Banshee was as surprised as everyone else when she promptly quieted. She looked up at the large human.

"Good girl. Can you sit?"

The large human made a gesture with his hand. He needn't have gestured. For that matter he needn't have spoken. She understood what he wanted from his tone and energy. And since he hadn't demanded it, she obliged. Settled down onto her haunches.

"Good girl. Wait."

Banshee waited. The pack gaped. Stan smirked.

Bring in a badder cop.

"Won't be much longer," Stan said. "Just one last thing to take care of, then we'll be on our way and the cops'll come for you."

Stan approached the incinerator. When flesh is exposed to those temperatures, the meats and liquids are consumed, leaving only bone. Which does not burn. Ashes sent to loved ones of those departed are not ashes at all. They are pulverized, powdered bone.

Stan swept the skeletal remains into a pile. The incinerator hadn't been emptied in a while. He noted bones of at least three other breeds mixed in with Chopper's. Two skulls happened to tumble out. One a pittie, the other Chopper's. They rolled to rest, side by side.

Stan found he couldn't breathe.

He picked up the pittie skull, left Chopper's on the floor, turned on the grinder. Scooped in the bones of dogs and human. They crunched and cracked, mixing into a mingled powder.

He faced the pack. They had watched in silent horror the whole time. As he snatched up Chopper's skull, something glinted in the jaw. He dug his fingers in, pulled and pried. A misshapen ingot popped loose.

He held up the melted and rehardened golden grill.

"In case you needed a reminder."

He tossed the metal to the floor. It bounced and clanged. The pack whimpered. He tucked Chopper's skull under one arm, hefted the cold, stiffened corpse of Raptor over his other, grabbed a shovel, and stalked outside.

Banshee followed.

Stan found a pristine piece of earth under an ancient tree about a hundred yards from the compound. Tossed Chopper's skull unceremoniously to the ground. Laid Raptor down oh so gently. Began to dig. Banshee watched Stan give Raptor a proper burial. Then he kicked the skull into the freshly turned earth. Wrapped his hands around the handle of the shovel. No gloves. He'd catch hell from Adler and Price. Stan was adamant about protecting one's physical integrity. But he wanted to feel this.

Stan brought the shovel down like a homesteader splitting logs to feed the hearth through the brutal winter. As though his life depended on it. Over and over.

Banshee watched. And waited.

Stan felt blisters rising on his palms. He welcomed them. The sweat on his skin steamed in the sharp air. He struck and struck. The shovel clanged. The skull cracked. Stan struck and struck.

Between strikes, he spoke names.

"Scott."

crack

"Philly."

clang

"Wilkerson."

clang

"Devonte."

crack

The names were prayers. The names were curses. The names fractured the skull and broke it apart.

27

"Jackson. Victoria. Mahoney."

Banshee didn't understand the words but she felt how each word tore itself out of him. Felt how his pain shifted through the color spectrum from agony to guilt to rage to helplessness.

"AJAX!"

That word... it came from a place in him so deep and so raw that a place in her responded. Because dogs aren't descended from wolves. Dogs and wolves are cousins. They share a common ancestor. It was a curious and brave few of these ancestors who first approached the two-legged hunter-gatherers and their miraculous cooking fires. The descendants of these few, over centuries and millennia, became dogs. Dogs and humans evolved together, intertwined. Dogs are the only animal that look humans directly in the eye, that turn to humans for comfort before others of their own species. Dogs and humans don't exist in their modern incarnations without each other.

So when Stan yelled "AJAX!" and brought the shovel down for the final time, Banshee's deepest agonies instinctively vibrated at the same frequency. She recalled her puppies, all of them torn from her so small. She didn't remember them in any way a human would understand. She couldn't picture them. They didn't have names or even personalities. But they each had smells, that most visceral of the senses.

And now she smelled this human. His pain. His openness. She wanted to lick his face. But she dare not. Waiting for him was one thing. Bonding with him was another.

It would cost her too much.

28

Stan stopped.

His hands wept with blisters. His face was striped with sweat and tears and snot.

He had stripped off his shirt somewhere around "Mahoney," that arrogant Irish firecracker with her unruly head of red hair and tenacious spirit. The best Warrant Officer he'd ever worked with. Felled in some desert hellhole as she ran back into a burning apartment building from which she'd just pulled three terrified children. "There's one boy left in there, I got him!" she had yelled over her shoulder. The enemy mortar had hit the moment she disappeared back into the building. Stan and those three children still communicated. One was studying medicine. One joined the military. One became a dancer.

Hell wasn't a place. Stan knew this well. Hell was just memory. Replayed and unchangeable.

The skull was wrecked. He'd never be able to pulverize it into powder, not when it was sitting on soft soil. But it was obliterated. He winced through his raw palms and turned the dirt over a few times, mingling the shards of Chopper's skull with the myriad dog bones resting in the earth.

A soft, keening howl shivered his arms. He looked down. Banshee stood beside him, her muzzle lifted high, that timeless sound unfurling out of her, exhaling his pain. She returned to silence. Huffed once through her nose. Turned and walked away without a backward glance.

Stan recognized her wisdom. Picked up his discarded t-shirt, followed Banshee back to the compound, headed to the bathroom to wash and clean and bandage.

Back at the grave, the ancient tree stretched its roots into the dirt, and waited. In time, grass and flowers would blanket those souls.

29

STAN DID a final walk-through of the Pit. Erased all traces of the Troupe. Dumped the last of the jerky and power bars and bottled water in a pile for the zip-tied pack. Took all the powdered bone from the grinder and spread it around the dog run. Ashes to ashes.

Banshee followed him step for step.

Stan paused by his Subaru and slipped on his shades.

"Headed your way. Send the cavalry."

He opened the passenger door.

"C'mon, girl."

Banshee tilted her head. Assessed.

"Up you go."

She sprang into the front seat.

He got behind the wheel. Executed a three-point turn. Eased down the path. Noticed Banshee pressing her nose against the window, leaving wet, modern-art smears on the glass. He flicked the switch. She startled as the window lowered, then stuck her head out.

She marveled. The sounds! The *smells*! The air swishing

through her fur and around her ears. Who knew the world was this wide and alive??

She pulled her head back in and looked at Stan. Eye to eye, as only dogs do.

He braked them to a gentle stop. The engine idled. Stan waited.

Banshee tilted her head. Her mouth opened. Her tongue flapped out sideways. She panted lightly, open and trusting.

Stan grinned. "Well look at that. You do have a Rottie smile." He reached over and scratched under her chin. She presented her throat just so, so he could hit the exact right spot. She sighed. "Good girl, Banshee."

She looked at him. Assessed. He looked back. Waited. She stood in the seat, put one massive paw on the center console, and stretched forward. Her ridiculously long tongue flicked out and licked his face. Once. Twice. Three times.

Stan couldn't help himself. He giggled like a little boy.

In that moment, because he asked nothing of her, she gave him everything. Opened her heart in that way that only dogs know how to do. And she understood for the first time what it meant—what it *felt* like—to be man's best friend.

"Good girl."

There was nothing she wouldn't do for this human.

Banshee sat back down in her seat, stuck her head back out the window. Stan wiped his face, still giggling. He released the brake and they resumed their slow descent of the mountain. The tires flung up dust that hung in the sunlight, waiting to return to the earth.

ACKNOWLEDGMENTS

All my thanks to Scott Mann, Denee Lortz, the Rabbit Room, everyone who voted on the cover at 99Designs, Mom, and the team at K9 Korral.

ABOUT THE AUTHOR

Jason Cannon is an award-winning theatre artist and teacher. He has an MFA in Directing, a Masters in Drama, and a quarter-century in professional theatre.

When not on stage or in rehearsal Jason devours every Lee Child, James Rollins, Mark Dawson, Vince Flynn, Brad Thor, and Randy Wayne White book in the cosmos.

As an actor Jason has portrayed everything from a rapping dinosaur to a robot and from a hitman to Hamlet. He has written plays about J.R.R. Tolkien and Aesop, directed plays about hiccuping dragons and foul-mouthed puppets, and once while improvising he was attacked by a stage light.

He lives in Florida just a holler from the Gulf with his partner Rebecca and their two silly pups, Gaia and Odin. He makes a killer key lime pie and runs lots of 10Ks and half-marathons.

Jason believes storytelling in all its forms—whether seen on the stage or read on a page—has the power not only to entertain but also to comfort, provoke, and inspire us to be better humans.

If you enjoyed *THE UNDERSTUDY*, please consider leaving a review. They are super helpful!

Jason is also available as a teacher, speaker, and emcee.

Learn more about Jason at jason-cannon.com.

You can check out the first book in the TROUPE series —*GHOST LIGHT*—and watch for the next two stories in the TROUPE series—*BLACKOUT* and *RULE OF THREE*—at ibis-books.com.

ALSO BY JASON CANNON

THE TROUPE SERIES

The Understudy

Ghost Light

PLAYS

Wheelchair Chicken

Last Rights

Old Enough to Know Better

The Eagle and Child: J.R.R. Tolkien and C.S. Lewis

Windsor Live!

Aesop's Greatest Hits

FREE PREVIEW

Turn the page for an extended free preview of *GHOST LIGHT*, the first story in the thrilling TROUPE Series.

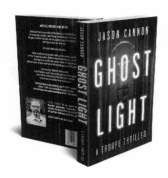

1

Thousands of feet thunderstormed into the pavement. Home-made signs stabbed at the overcast sky. The crowd throbbed.

A bullhorn called. *"No Justice...!!"*

The throng responded one-throated. "NO PEACE!!"

"No Justice...!!"

"NO PEACE!!"

The young white man walking along the outskirts had no interest in this mob's brand of "peace."

He would leave such a scar. He would slash wounds down to the genes. Children of those who survived today would grow up looking over their shoulders, wondering if his ghost was creeping up on them.

Finally. It was his time. All was in place.

He had underestimated the turnout to this protest—who knew there were this many porch monkeys, beaners, and chinks in this town??—so working his way toward the head of the crowd had put him seven minutes behind schedule.

But talk about your silver linings. The march itself started late for the same reason. He made up his time in no time. And the swelling numbers ultimately meant a greater sacrifice.

With everyone so focused on their self-absorbed chanting and whiny bitching for "equality," no one saw him slipping his perfectly primed packages into public trash cans. Receptacles eager to shred into shrapnel.

His primary targets led the march. The half-breed Congresswoman and the Judas Congressman. A few minutes more and the blast radius would embrace them.

He shivered in disgust even as he savored his impending immortality. The crowd was such that even on the edges he couldn't avoid the occasional shoulder bump with a filthy skin. It made him uncomfortable. And his discomfort made him furious.

Their stupid homemade signs. Their false fury. Their inability to see the world as it actually was… sick and dying, in need of *curing*.

He suddenly couldn't breathe. He found sanctuary in a pocket of space created by a consignment store's entryway. Watched the horde stomp past.

A ribbon of White people swirled through the black and brown mass. He snarled inside. Traitors. How could they forfeit their birthright? Snowflakes indeed were White.

Which of them would die today?

It didn't actually matter to the young man, but it was a fun thought experiment to pick out individuals from the oblivious throng, see if he could tell which were marked for martyrdom.

The power hummed in his marrow. When the moment came… all that would be required… a simple press of finger to phone…

boom

boom

boom boom

boom

Anticipation saturated him.

He forged back out into the crush, working upstream toward the final targeted trash can. Arrived. Pretended to tie his shoe. Cased the corner. Unzipped his previously bulging backpack. Dropped his last IED. Re-zipped. The bag flopped flaccid over his shoulder, spent and happy.

Soon. So soon. The world would see. And understand his cause. And know his name. His *true* name.

SPEARHEAD.

2

A FEW MONTHS EARLIER, MANHATTAN

"What is acting?"

Gideon Price pulled a chair to the center of the small studio stage and sat. Twelve students faced him, most of them a diverse batch of 20-somethings, along with two Black women in their mid-30s who appeared to be friends, a Caucasian married couple in that 50ish range, and a grandfatherly, mustachioed white fellow.

They all remained silent, waiting for someone else to speak first. Gideon re-rolled a sleeve of his lightweight button-down.

"It's not a trick question. And at the risk of starting our time together with a cliche, there are no wrong answers."

Gideon waited, smiling pleasantly, his hands casually folded in his lap. After a few moments, a young Latinx man flung up his hand. Gideon nodded.

"Pretending to be someone else?"

"Sure, yeah."

The married couple both raised their hands. Gideon again nodded.

The couple whispered back and forth, acting out the timeless relation- ship negotiation of who ought to go first. The husband finally insisted the wife take the lead.

"Telling a story?"

"OK, good."

She sat back, pleased. The husband leaned forward. "Becoming rich and famous?"

The class chuckled. Gideon loved it when a student got the first laugh in a first class. That always set the group instinctively at ease.

"For a very cloistered few, absolutely." More chuckles, and now hands flew up all over.

"Mr. Price, what do you mean by cloistered few?" asked an eager young white man in the front row.

"Please, Gideon is fine. Here's what I mean by 'few.' A very tiny percentage of professional actors make their living solely from acting. A somewhat less tiny percentage make their living by cobbling together various performing gigs, everything from voice-overs to theme parks to TV commercials, with some live theatre thrown in. Most have one or more—cue the scary music—*survival jobs*."

More chuckles, looser and louder. The young man followed up.

"So acting is actually... any type of performing?"

"Well now that's a different conversation. There's the art, and there's the business. Whatever the medium, all acting comes back to the same core principles. Plenty more on that later."

The young man was not to be deterred. "And cloistered?"

"That one's easier. If your face is everywhere, if your name is currency, the pressure mounts. The expectations grow. You never leave your house without sunglasses and a cap pulled low. Your private life becomes public. Wealth and fame—as many celebrities attest—end up holding you hostage."

"Sounds good to me!" the husband chimed in. And the class ripped off its first good laugh. Gideon smiled inwardly. He never tired of watching a group of strangers evolve into community.

One of the 30-something friends gasped. "I got it!"

Everyone startled and looked her way. Gideon lopsided a grin and pointed. "Remind me your name?"

"Imani."

"What is it you got, Imani?"

"Who you remind me of!"

Everyone swung their attention to Gideon, probing with keen interest the contours of his face.

"Ho boy. Moment of truth. Do tell."

"Mr. Price—I mean, Gideon—you are a dead ringer for Daredevil!" A few voices went "oooooh!" and "yeeeeah." A couple others went "huh." The mustache went "Who?"

Imani clapped her hands. "Same brown hair, same dark eyebrows, you're definitely taller though."

"Wasn't that Ben Affleck?" the husband asked, squinting at Gideon's face.

Imani was appalled. "Not the *movie*. The TV show!"

Imani's friend—Gideon recalled her name as *Aniyah*—spoke over Imani's squeals. "Don't get her started. She's watched the whole series like five times."

Gideon let the delighted chatter play out. This good-natured moment was his cue for the first "inspirational teacher" monologue. He stood, ran a hand through his apparently Davedevil-y hair. The laughter came in for a gentle landing. He spoke.

"At its most fundamental, acting is simply behaving truthfully within imaginary circumstances. Note that 'truthfully' is a much larger word than 'realistically.' Also note that it's 'behaving,' not 'feeling.' It is, after all, called ACTING. To act. To do. Feelings, yes, are key and we'll get to them. But if your feelings do not manifest into action? If the audience doesn't see it or hear it? They won't get it. True on stage. True in life."

"Sorta sounds like 'faith without works is dead,'" offered the Latinx man.

"Useful comparison, Alfonso, yeah. I've never woven the Apostle Paul into my acting class before, but sure. Feelings. Beliefs. Faith. Points of view whether political or moral, if they don't manifest into action, they're just... thoughts. Air." Gideon's eyebrows furrowed. "Alfonso, I'm blanking... Is that from 'Galatians'?"

"Book of 'James,' baby!" Alfonso fist-pumped.

Chuckles as four pens and three pencils scratched madly. Two tablets and one smart book, perched on laps, click-clacked at competing words per minute. The thumbs of the eager young man took notes on his phone. The 70-something gentleman simply held up an old-school dictation recorder.

Gideon continued. "You will never master this craft. You will always have room to grow as an artist, because—hopefully —you will always be growing as a human being. You cannot separate the two. Another great definition of acting is that it is simply standing on stage naked and slowly turning around."

Gasps and snorts punctuated the giggling. Imani was the first gasper to catch up to the metaphor. "Oh my god I thought you meant literally." "No no, though actually I did have one role where I had to, um, fully de-robe on stage. It's actually... well, intoxicating and empowering."

"Oh reeeeeally?" Imani said, leaning forward with a glint in her eye.

Her ornery curiosity wildfired through the other students.

Gideon held up his hands. "OK OK, my bad, not the story for class one."

The wife reached back and patted the pouting Imani's knee. "Don't worry, dear, we'll get that story."

Gideon got the class back on track. "You must cultivate vulnerability and a thick skin. You must cede control while maintaining control. You must find yourself in every character, and every character inside yourself. If that sounds like a lot, just remember this: you must simply stand on stage and tell the truth."

"Is it really that easy?" A new voice. She was late-20s, with piercing slate eyes, dark brown skin, and a shorn scalp.

"It's Rheia, right?"

"Yep."

"It's the hardest easy thing in the world."

3

AN HOUR LATER, the class returned from a quick break, chattering excitedly about the physical and vocal warm-ups, the elocution exercises, the tongue twisters, the icebreaker games designed to help everyone learn each other's names.

"I know a lot of that probably felt silly," Gideon said. "But silliness is vulnerability, and vulnerability is necessary if you want to act. So the exercises and warm-ups have a dual purpose. They stretch and strengthen your physical and vocal apparatus, and they free you from the shackles of ego."

The older gentleman spoke up. "But don't you have to have an ego if you're an actor? Or any artist? Aren't you saying 'Hey look at me! Look at my work!'"

"Good point, Marcel. This goes back to the fame idea, yeah? But for every famous artist you know, there are thousands, tens of thousands, grinding away in anonymity, going daily to the smithy of their souls to forge something meaningful with their creativity."

Gideon sat down, leaned forward conspiratorially. The students instinctively settled.

"At the end of the day, the mission of the actor, of any artist, is simply to move the body of work forward. Ninety-nine-point-nine-nine-nine percent of the world will never know my name. Never see me perform, or read my plays, or—unlike you wise few—take my class."

Smiles flickered. Gideon took his time, making deliberate eye contact with each of the extraordinary humans across from him.

"The number of Shakespeares in the world? The ones who can change the world from the top down? That number is infinitesimal... and they don't do that on their own. We are all interconnected. There are as many molecules of air in one breath of air as there are breaths of air in the entire atmosphere. There are as many molecules of water in one glass of water as there are glasses of water in all the Earth's oceans. Shakespeare doesn't happen without every other actor and playwright plying their craft before him. That old chestnut: bloom where you're planted? Well, the field is only a field if each individual blooms. The random Shakespeare-tree that grows out of that field... its very tree- ness is only apparent because of the field around it. The tree owes itself to the field."

Gideon leaned back.

"So... does my work not matter? If I only ever am part of the field?"

He watched as each student contemplated the question. Some eyes went up to the ether. Some down into memory. The married couple gazed at each other, and Gideon saw them squeeze hands. He continued.

"It's up to me to believe that what I do has meaning. Others can decide if it's 'good' or not, whatever, I will never please everyone. But I can contribute. Even just a single verse, right? For you Whitman fans. What will your verse be?"

Gideon noted that Imani had put her arm around Aniyah,

who was working a handkerchief between her fingers, pulling and wrapping and clutching. Gideon caught Aniyah's eyes. They were brimming. *You are seen,* he thought, sending as much gentle warmth toward her as he could. Whatever she received, she nodded, took a deep breath, eased her grip on the hanky.

"You know during the pandemic a poll was taken and the general population listed 'artist' as the least essential job in our society. 'Essen- tial.' I have to wonder how many of those polled only maintained their sanity through quarantine because they listened to music. Read a book. Watched a movie. Consumed art."

The class nodded. Gideon found he couldn't sit any longer.

"Art makes it easier to breathe. Art may not be how we stay alive, but it's why we live at all." He paced. He vibrated. Calm guru fired up into impassioned prophet.

"Do you remember every single meal from last month? Of course not. Well, maybe if you're journaling or food planning, but you'd still have to double-check your records. Never mind, here's the point—do you need to eat every day? Absolutely. Even if you can't recall *what* you ate, you know that you *did.* The same with art. So while food helps our bodies grow and fuels our daily activities, art helps our minds and hearts and humanity grow, fuels our daily evolution. Art is food for the soul."

Gideon prowled the small stage.

"And this is why art is *essential*—it provides context, it carves meaning, it gives us a framework to make sense of our lives and a world that so often seems senseless. And as we learn to create art we learn to see artistry in those around us. Theatre happens... all the time... all around you."

Gideon paused, a conductor suspended between notes.

"You know... just last week... in a bar of all places... I saw what I could only describe as a 'performance.' As powerful and true as anything I've ever seen on stage."

"Well isn't all the world a stage?" Rheia asked.

"And all the men and women merely players?" Marcel finished.

"Indeed, Mr. Wigglestick says as much through the voice of the melancholy Jaques," Gideon conceded. "There's a hopelessness in there, a dismissiveness that has always gnawed at me. I want to believe in theatre as something aspirational, and last week in the bar..."

Gideon hesitated. He was way off-script, and the class knew it. "I'm honestly... it was just a bar fight."

"A bar fight??" Rheia prodded.

"Yes. But it was... more?"

"What bar?"

"The Bear and Fawn, just over on 46th."

Several nods of recognition, a few quizzical eyebrows. And the timeless, hushed insistence of the campfire.

Tell us the story.

He inhaled their rapt attention and started to carve the narrative. "I was having a well-deserved bourbon after a two-show day."

4

GIDEON WATCHED it all unfold in the mirror behind the bar.

A 20-something Black guy playing at being dapper in a white suit had sucker-punched his pool opponent, another 20-something Black guy in jeans and a Henley. The sounds of the punch and Henley's clatter to the floor had frozen every patron mid-bite.

White Suit crowed, "Yeah! That's what's you *get!*" His two gym- thick wingmen hooted. They high-fived and low-fived. Henley's friend helped him up, blood from his now crooked nose staining the billiard felt black.

No one moved. Not the trio of cool dudes hitting on the girls at the dartboards. Not the booth full of mud-streaked amateur rugby toughs. Not the bartender. Not Gideon.

White Suit and his wingmen strutted toward the exit. The bar held its breath, ashamed of inaction, but anticipating the relief that would come when the proverbial bullies left the playground.

How she appeared Gideon would never remember. But suddenly there she was: average height, tight black ponytail, bangs, large opaque sunglasses, dark jeans, dark jacket over a basic T, skin tone that a theatrical agent would call "ethnically ambiguous." Everything about her—and looking back Gideon realized this was intentional—just *blended*.

The only reason she stuck out was that unlike everyone else in the bar she was standing between White Suit and the door. Her hands idly twirled a wooden pool rack.

"Why did you hit him?"

Gideon blinked. The voice that came out of the deceptively average woman was rich and resonant. Like a judge. Or a queen. Or an empress. He could have sworn even the lights shifted.

He glanced around. The Woman's blunt query had transformed the air hockey, the stools, the four-tops, the coasters, the neon, even the strangely muffled blatherings of some play-by-play guy on the TV... into a theatre. And Gideon would know; he had just held center stage as King Henry the Fifth an hour ago.

Gideon turned his attention back to the Woman, acutely aware he was now a member of an audience.

White Suit swiveled his head back and forth, sensitive to the shift in the air but unsure what it meant. Every eye in the bar was on him, an unwitting actor in a play with no clue what his next line was.

Gideon tasted a familiar growing electricity in the air.

The Woman cocked her head to one side, the triangle in her hands still slowly spinning.

"I ask sincerely. Why did you hit him?"

White Suit and his buds in turn cocked their heads, like dogs hearing the word "treat." White Suit opened his mouth. Closed it. Looked to his left. His friend gave a perplexed shrug.

"Come now," the Woman continued in that voice that wove through the bar. "We all are curious. It appeared that other young man won fair and square, yes?" She glanced past White Suit. Henley hesitantly nodded, not wanting more attention from the bullies.

"So I ask again, on behalf of everyone here who was just looking to have a good time tonight... why did you hit him?"

White Suit casually picked up a pool cue, buying time. What response could get him out of this without losing face? He chuckled audibly and looked around, gauging the audience's reaction.

No one believed him.

An ageless and universal story. Ego at its most primal. Either White Suit would yield—unlikely—or he would escalate.

White Suit's chuckle smeared itself into a sneer. His two strongmen inhaled and drew themselves up. Gideon felt his arms break out in gooseflesh, and he sensed the audience collectively lean forward.

"OK, Miss. You're right. I sucker punched that asshole." White Suit's voice in comparison to the Woman's, even though he was trying to sound patronizing and macho, came off reedy and thin. He knew it. He tried to snort. "But so what? You his babysitter or something?"

No one as much as tittered. So he glanced to his side, and his wingmen obligingly guffawed.

"I've never met him." The Woman's voice again froze time. "You should now apologize."

White Suit studied her closely, bouncing the pool cue in his hands. "You've got some balls," he drawled.

"I see you failed anatomy." The audience didn't know whether to giggle or gasp. "There's no dodging this, gentlemen. You owe this man an apology."

"Whatever. C'mon, T, move her out of the way. We're out."

The smaller of the two wingmen, T apparently, stepped

toward the Woman. "Smaller" was relative. Next to her he was a hulk.

Gideon suddenly wondered why no one was joining the Woman. Why HE wasn't joining.

T stopped short of the Woman, raised his hands palms out in a sorry- but-I-have-to-do-this gesture. "I don't wanna hurt ya," he said.

"That's kind of you, T. I don't want to hurt you either."

The bar choked on another giggle-gasp. She laid the rack on the nearest table.

"But if your hand touches me, I will break it." The Woman said this matter-of-factly, devoid of threat or anger. It was immutable. She may as well have said "Today is Saturday."

T looked back at White Suit.

"Get her out of the way! We're leaving."

T nodded, turned back to the Woman, gave an oversized shrug. "I don't hit ladies, so I'm just gonna..." His beefy hand reached toward her shoulder. "C'mon now."

When Gideon recalled this moment, he would see it as a series of still images, like panels in a comic book. First panel, T's fingers making contact with the Woman's jacket.

Second panel, T's eyes wide in surprise as he sees his hand in the Woman's vice-tight grip.

Third panel, T on his knees howling, the Woman torquing his wrist to an improbable degree.

Fourth panel, a close-up of fingers jutting at odd angles, the words "CRACK" and "SNAP" written in huge, technicolor font.

Fifth panel, T curled on the ground, cradling his hand, the Woman standing over him, cool and unperturbed, a text bubble floating above her head:

"You should learn to hit ladies."

5

THE STUDENTS STARED AT HIM, agog.

"There is NO WAY she said that!" said the eager young fellow. *Evan, Evan, Evan,* Gideon thought to himself; memorizing names on day one was always a challenge. Evan spluttered on, "That's like what you hear in a movie."

Gideon held up his hands. "No, I swear. That's exactly what she said. And that's why I'm saying I felt like I was at a play. This woman... she was *performing* for everyone in the bar."

Evan was a dog with a bone. "So what happened next?"

"Act Two will have to wait, I've used up more time than I meant to, let's get to work. Everybody up, grab a partner!" The class grumbled good-naturedly as they moved to the stage and paired off.

"Mirroring is a foundational theatre exercise. It's been around since the first baby mimicked the first mommy's facial expressions. Partners, face each other, a couple feet apart. Choose an A and a B. A's raise your hands?"

Half a dozen hands went up.

"B's?"

The half dozen hands swapped for six of the other.

"Great. B's will start. All you're going to do is slowly move. Arms, legs, hands, head. Tilt forward, backward, sideways. Extreme facial expressions, wild fingers. But the goal is for your partner to be able to mirror you, to match precisely every movement you make. Your goal is not to fool your partner, that's easy, and funny only the first time. You want to lock in together so that an audience watching wouldn't be able to tell who's leading and who's following. And go."

The students began to move. The room filled with giggles and exclamations. Some pairs connected right off, while others struggled, but as the exercise went on the room got quieter and more focused.

"Now A's take the lead. Again, the goal is to appear as if no one is leading, that you two are moving in concert."

Gideon floated around the room, making small comments and suggestions, but also flipping mental flashcards, reviewing names and the information shared during introductions.

Here was Evan, the eager lad just out of acting conservatory and taking his first professional class in the big city. He exuded a sweet hope that Gideon hoped showbiz wouldn't stomp out of him too soon.

Evan was paired with Alfonso, who had proudly declared that his parents were immigrants from Zapopan, Mexico, and that he was taking the class to further his drag career. "Next time 'Salsa Verde' takes the stage, I'll be sure to let you all know!"

Gideon smiled inwardly as he saw Marcel, the oldest student in the group, paired with Emma, the youngest. Marcel was Polish, a retired surgeon who donated a big chunk of his time to training up first responders. Emma, soft-spoken and petite, wasn't even twenty but had seen *Wicked* when she was a kid and had dreamt of Broadway ever since.

The Forths, Dan and Joan, both worked in publishing, and were both each other's second spouse. They had met via an old-school print personal ad. The youngsters couldn't believe what they hearing. "Is that like Tinder?" Alfonso had asked, inadvertently setting Dan up for a punchline he had clearly used dozens of times. "No, son, if you swipe right on a newspaper you just smear the ink!"

Aniyah and Imani introduced themselves together, Imani doing most of the speaking. They had been friends since childhood. Imani did something in finance, and Aniyah had just moved in to Imani's guest room after life took a couple hard turns back in Detroit. They were taking the class as something fun to do together, and Gideon intuited also to help Aniyah find new friends and move forward.

Two aspiring actresses, like Evan just out of school, had immediately clicked and were mirroring like their lives and future Tony awards depended on it. Kaida was third-generation Japanese—"My name means 'little dragon'! Isn't that awesome??"—while Tosha's parents had moved to New York from Moscow when she was twelve. She wanted nothing more than to rip out the lingering Russian roots from her English. "No audience believes Russian Gypsy Rose Lee."

And the final pair was Rasheed and Rheia. Rasheed was the first in his Pakistani family to graduate from college, but four years into a frustrating TV and film career that had seen him play various versions of "Middle Eastern Terrorist" and not much else. He was desperate to expand his skills and land some juicier roles.

Rheia didn't reveal much but did warn that because she traveled a lot for work she might have to miss the occasional class. She had sat a few seats away from the main group and rarely moved or spoke. *Observer*, Gideon thought. And behind those high privacy walls, he guessed she possessed an acute b.s. detector.

"Great work, everyone! Take your seats. Any observations from that exercise?"

The discussion, as usual, focused on eyes being windows to the soul, the feeling of connectivity once you took it seriously, overcoming self- consciousness, becoming hypersensitive to the actual mechanics of how your muscles move your body, and—

"Releasing ego," Rheia said, beating Gideon to the punch.

"Go on."

"When I'm leading the mirror, it's not at all about what I do. It's about taking care of my partner. If Rasheed messed up, that actually was on me. Even though I was technically leading, I was serving something bigger than myself."

Eleven pairs of eyes swung Gideon's way. Rheia had nailed it, he had nothing to add, so he gave a confirming nod-shrug. Notes were furiously scribbled and typed.

But Rheia sat sphinx-like. Gideon met her unwavering gaze, and they suddenly had their own mirroring moment... was he assessing her assessing him? Or the other? Or both?

Tosha abruptly piped up. "Hey! We are still having a couple minutes—"

"—so can you tell the rest of your story?" Kaida finished.

Universal clamor.

"OK, OK. If this story takes me past time, you can leave if you've gotta catch your train or whatever."

"I still can't believe she said 'You should learn to hit ladies,'" Evan muttered. "So badass."

6

Had the Woman even moved? The amount of violence performed in those couple of seconds left the bar dumb-founded. The rack was back in her hands, idly spinning. White Suit and Wingman were staring at T, mouths agape. Gideon realized his mouth also hung open and closed it with a click.

The bar started to murmur. Gideon saw White Suit's knuckles turning white as he tightened his grip on the pool cue. *He's getting ready to attack,* Gideon thought.

But before White Suit could inhale to bark his big boy challenge, the Woman spoke. Still calm. Still in command.

"I want everyone here to note that actions have consequences. I have not behaved aggressively. I have simply stood up for someone else, and offered space for an apology multiple times. Unfortunately I also had to defend myself, though I gave fair warning. You all bear witness."

She turned her full attention to White Suit. His breathing accelerated. Wingman synced up, his massive bulk quivering.

"So. Gentleman. A second chance. How often do those come around? An apology, an offering from your wallet for this young man's urgent care visit, and I'll hold the door open for you. T will need medical attention as well."

The stillness pulled bowstring taut, twanged by T's occasional whimpering. Somewhere behind Gideon, a woman tried to suppress a cough. He again noted the oddity of the televisions having hushed.

White Suit shook his head and clucked his tongue. Gideon tensed.

Here it comes.

"What's your name, anyway?" White Suit said in a transparent attempt to catch the Woman off guard. The rack came to rest in her hands.

White Suit whipped his pool cue back like a baseball bat, a home run hitter trying to end the game. In reality, his cue hadn't even reached its rear apex before the Woman had stepped forward and pistoned a jab with the triangle.

The shortest distance between any two points, after all, is a straight line.

White Suit's head snapped back. His hands spasmed, releasing the cue. He staggered, widening his feet to keep his balance. Football being a more apt metaphor than baseball for this particular moment, the Woman's leg slash through a perfect punter's pendulum. The lowest part of her shin landed precisely between White Suit's legs, lifting him off the ground. White Suit and his pool cue hit the floor simultaneously.

Several patrons now finally moved. The four rugby friends stood and looked primed to jump in and rumble now that the Woman had subdued two of the three.

Wingman sensed it, too. All those hours flinging weights at the gym had in no way prepared him for this particular circumstance.

"*Third* chance. Seriously, you never *ever* get those."

Wingman looked around. Did the math. Reached into his

pocket and pulled out his wallet. Clutched it in his sweaty hand.

"Go ahead. Whatever cash you've got in there, that'll be just fine. Put it on the pool table. All good. Then take care of your friends."

One of the rugby dudes chimed in. "Yeah! That's right! That's what YOU get!" The bar trembled, other throats started to clear. But Gideon could tell the Woman didn't want a mob. The audience needed to stay the audience.

"No." The Woman's voice crackled with authority. Rugby Dude stepped back. "You are late to this party. Save it for next time."

"Next time?" Gideon asked the question impulsively. He felt the spotlight swing his way. The attention was terrifying and delicious, as electric a rush as he had ever felt on stage. The Woman's eyes—invisible behind the sunglasses—bored into him.

Wingman, his hackles up from Rugby Dude's taunt, in the end could not swallow his pride. Taking advantage of Gideon's inadvertent distraction, he lunged a huge left-hook at the Woman's head.

She slither-stepped aside. As the fist harmlessly sailed by, the Woman snapped her heel into Wingman's knee. He tumbled. In a blink she had lassoed his neck with the triangle, slid behind him, and pulled the triangle garrote-taut into his throat. He choked and flailed, but she was implacable. She spoke over Wingman's gasps.

"We live in a fallen world, my friend."

Wingman's eyes rolled up in his head. She released him and he thumped unconscious to the floor next to White Suit and T. The Woman turned to Gideon, not a hair out of place.

"There's always a next time."

7

EVEN AFTER GOING OVER TIME, the students hadn't wanted to disperse. They were going to be a tight-knit group.

Evan, predictably, bent Gideon's ear into a pretzel.

"No way no way no WAY! She spoke directly to you? She dropped another Hollywood-perfect line on you??"

"That's how it happened, best I can remember."

Gideon was cleaning up, checking that no one had left anything behind, turning off lights and a/c. Evan babbled on even as everyone else evaporated into the steamy New York night.

"So did anyone call the cops? Did she say anything else to you? Did you get her name? DUDE did you get her number??"

Gideon set the ghost light, slung his well-traveled Osprey backpack over his shoulders, and placated Evan best he could. No, no one had called the cops, she hadn't said anything else, no name, definitely no number. He led Evan outside, locked the deadbolt, shook hands.

"Thanks Mr. Price, I mean Gideon, I mean that was awesome, can't wait for next class!"

"Glad to hear it, Evan. Good work tonight."

Gideon watched Evan whip out his cell and hurry away. He stood a moment. Took in the sudden solitude. Took out the final images of that night in the bar. He hadn't shared the denouement with the class, it sounded too bizarre...

Wingman thumps to the floor. The Woman turns to Gideon. "There's always a next time." The TVs suddenly blare. The lights flash blinding full. Even the CD jukebox in the corner thunders to life.

And in the chaos, the Woman disappears. Gideon glimpses her slipping out the exit, leaving White Suit, T, and Wingman in various states of brokenness on the beer-stained floor. He leaps after her, pressing through the surge of patrons. The cacophony, the crowd, the chaos, he fights through them all to reach the door.

He springs out onto the sidewalk. Looks left. Right. Left again.

She's gone.

He also hadn't told the class that he had gone back to the Bear and Fawn every night since, hoping the Woman would reappear. Or that his post-show bourbon that night had been a triple, and that in recent days those triples had doubled.

He couldn't even admit it to himself, so how could he tell the class?

His facade crumbled. He deflated. He slumped against the door. The city throbbed and honked and moaned.

His pockets were full of masks. He wadded up "charming teacher" and stuffed it in with the others.

Go home, Gideon. A nightcap, a couple chapters of the latest Neal Stephenson, hit the hay, all good.

To be haunted simply means you haven't let go of the past.

But what if the past won't let go of you? Does that make *you* the ghost? That's how Gideon felt, like a translucent wisp. But for a few weeks, during rehearsal for *Henry Five*, he had been able to pack the past away into the back of the tiny closet in his tiny sublet. No time to think, in the theater all day and night, surrounded by like-minded artists, nowhere to be but the present.

Bliss.

Losing himself in the show, anonymous in the giant city. For the first time in a long time, his sleep rejuvenated. No sweat. No dreams. No tangled blankets. Exactly what Gideon had hoped for, escaping to New York.

Just go the hell home.

But then the show had opened. And Gideon found himself with time. So much time. Too much time and too few masks. Anonymity rotted from blessing to burden. Solitude curdled into loneliness. So much *time.* His sleep evaporated. The past bounded out of the closet, too bulky to stuff in his pockets with the masks.

GO. HOME.

So the past became his only companion through morning minutes and afternoon hours. Every day a slogging struggle to get to the respite of the evening: fight call and make-up and costumes and co-stars and audience and bows and then...

The past. Hanging out at the stage door, eager for an autograph.

Gideon heaved himself onto the sidewalk, plodded toward the intersection where he'd have to decide how to kill time while Tuesday shed the mottled skin of Monday.

Can't kill time without injuring eternity.

The show still had two months to go in its run, but already he could feel the void looming beyond closing. What then? Where to?

Don't think about that, Gideon thought, knowing full well that the surest way to think about something is to tell yourself not to think about it. *Just go home, dammit.*

He reached the intersection. The Bear and Fawn beckoned a couple blocks this way, his sweaty bed that way.

The past gossiped at his side, oblivious.

Gideon pretended to deliberate.

The lights changed. Crosswalks filled. He turned this way, trudged yet again toward the Bear and Fawn. The Woman *had* something, *knew* something. And Gideon wanted it. He *needed* it, even if he couldn't articulate what it was. If only he could ask her.

And you know what? Even if she didn't appear, the bourbon would.

Wrapped up in the contemplation of this shittiest of win-wins, he didn't note the shadow that peeled itself off the wall and drift behind him step for step.

Gideon's adventure with the TROUPE begins in *GHOST LIGHT*! Visit ibis-books.com to purchase either the ebook or paperback, and see what else Ibis Books has to offer!

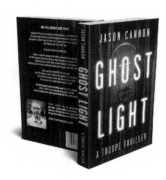

17813574R00093